The Nightmare Witch Saga
***

Lizzy Comes to Town

By: Mary Reason Theriot

Dedication

Without the love and support of my family and friends, I would not have pursued this new path in life. I would especially like to thank those that have proofread copy after copy, to give me their honest opinion of the books.

Theresa, thank you so much for your continued encouragement. Without you, some of the characters would not have "come to life."

To my wonderful husband Mat, your continued love and support mean the world to me.   I don't know what I would do without you in my life.   One of these nights I'm sure you will be able to sleep with both eyes closed. Eventually, I should run out of ideas… or maybe not. These books wouldn't be what they are without you pushing me forward.

To Little House of Edits for all of the wonderful work.

To my fans, I would like to offer a special thank you for your continued support.

This book is a work of fiction. Names, characters, places and incidents are the product of the author's imagination and are used fictitiously. Any resemblance to actual persons, living or dead, events or places are entirely coincidental.

ISBN-10: 1-945393-44-0
ISBN-13: 978-1-945393-44-0

Also Available by Mary Reason Theriot:

The Hideaway
The Traveler
Dr. Frankenstein
Above Suspicion
Horror in the Night
Echoes on the Bayou
Seven Deadly Sins
A Kiss So Deadly
A Deadly Combination
Seduced by Voodoo
CarnEvil of Souls
Redemption
Haunted Visions
Love's Embrace
Secrets

www.maryreasontheriot.com

My beloved Lizzy, I didn't want this life for you. I have learned the hard way that destiny isn't something you can run from, but something that should be embraced. Please forgive me for not telling you about our family.

You come from a long line of witches, dating back some two hundred years. When I renounced my heritage, I forbid my family from seeking me out. I wanted a normal life, and to live where no one knew anything about me.

My mistake has now left you unprotected. You have incredible powers inside of you; you must learn how to embrace these powers to keep you safe.

You must be careful, not all witches have good intentions, some practice dark magic, very dark magic. Unfortunately, some of those very witches are in our family. Be careful my beloved daughter.

Love,

Mom

Chapter 1

Blackwater Bayou, Louisiana 1829

Beneath an ancient oak tree a woman was huddled on the ground. Exhaustion consumed her body as black bark clung to her hair and damp dress.

Her fingers gripped the earth as sorrow over took her. Her vision blurred as tears filled her eyes. She heard the angry voices of the Acadians in the distance. She smelled the burning pitch of the torches. She stole too many children too close together. She had gone too far this time.

If only the spells didn't require the souls of innocent children, then maybe her presence would have gone unnoticed. But she had become too greedy. She was tired of being old.

Their tempers were high and feared that they planned to burn her alive. She must run, run far away from here.

A voice called out from in front of her, "What ails you woman?"

Crying, she replied, "Tis nothing but sorrow for the loss of my youth and beauty."

"You wish to have it once more?" he asked.

Nodding her head, she looked up to see a cloaked figure standing before her. She swallowed back her fear when she caught a glimpse of the face beneath the hood. It was that of a skeletal figure with glowing red eyes.

"I do," she replied.

A sly, swift gaze took in her appearance. The voice seemed to come from everywhere and yet nowhere as if it were not tethered to its actual form. "Thy have no family?"

"They are all gone. I live by myself along the bayou."

Helping her up off the ground, he said, "I can give you what you most desire, but be forewarned, it comes with a hefty price to pay."

She would give anything to have her beauty again. Anger filled her, burned deep in her veins at the mere thought of her faded beauty. "Alas, I have no money."

Looking deep into her eyes, he informed her, "What I require costs no money."

Beads of sweat rolled down her forehead, lines of concentration formed on her brow, "I would give my very soul for beauty."

A sinister laugh escaped from the creature's vile mouth, "Ah, that is exactly what I require."

"What of the townspeople? They are so near."

With a simple wave of his bony hand, he said, "Let them do with you what they will. Tis of no importance now."

As he disappeared into thin air, she screamed out, "Wait!"

Suddenly, she found herself surrounded by an angry mob. Waving pitchforks, they dragged her to the hangman's noose. "Old woman, you have gone too far! You will no longer practice your witchcraft here. There will be no more invading our homes and stealing our children in the middle of the night."

They hoisted her onto the galley, where the noose waited for her. She laughed as they tightened it around her neck. The fools were actually enjoying this. Rage filled her, a rage unlike any other that she has ever felt. A strange sensation crept up the length of her spine, spreading deep into the very core of her being. She looked over the crowd with a red glow to her irises. Crimson red blazed from her eyes as her cackling voice dripped with venom. "You think your noose will stop me? I will be back. I will come in your children's dreams, where you cannot protect them!"

She did not fear the death that awaited her, for it would only be her physical body that perished, her spirit would live on. In time, she would restore her body and once again return to seek revenge.

A man in the crowd called out, "Die witch!"

She turned to stare in the direction of the man. Sensing her angry glare, he quickly blended into the group of people around him in an attempt to vanish from her sight. *Pathetic mortals*, she thought to herself.

Another man in the crowd called out, "The witch has shown us her true evil. She has made a pact with the devil and must perish."

If her hands had not been bound, with the flick of her wrist she would shatter his neck. As she chanted, she continued to stare at the man. The palpable, tangible hatred he felt for her hung heavy in the air.

Her hatred for these people ran deep and even as she stood there, facing imminent death, she could sense their fear building. As she continued her chant, one of the villagers cried out, "She's cursing us. We must silence her."

It pleased her immensely to know that they would carry that fear for the rest of their miserable lives.

With a wave of his hand, the minister overseeing the hanging gave the order. As death embraced her, she vowed to return.

***

A burning pain started deep in the pit of her stomach and worked its way through her body. It felt as if her blood was boiling inside of her. Her skin mottled and her eyes pinched shut. She screamed out in pain, as if a hot knife had been stabbed deep into her heart. Her body began to tremble as a renewed strength moved into her. She rose from the earth in one fluid motion.

A flock of ravens flew frantically over the trees as a voice broke through the silent night. "I now have my payment. You may stand." When the cloaked creature opened his robe, soulless forms screamed out in agony as they reached out and grabbed her very soul where it joined them for all eternity.

The price had been paid, and would be paid over and over again. Revenge would be hers. The young and beautiful were doomed. This town would soon know what true fear was. Children would no longer have a peaceful night's sleep.

She had been granted the gift she desired, youth and beauty. He addressed her once more, "You now have the power of magic unlike any mortal has ever possessed." She watched as the lines on her hands vanished and the stains that had mottled her skin were no more.

As he disappeared into thin air, he reminded her, "Just remember that there is a price for your beauty."

Chapter 2

Fairy tales may depict the evil witch as an old hag, but you must remember that they are just that – fairy tales. Oftentimes evil came in the form of pure beauty.

Deep in the swamps of Louisiana lived the Chauchemar, or as she has recently become known as the Nightmare Witch. Anger burned in her veins, her need for revenge all consuming. She had been granted the power of youth and beauty by the devil himself, but it came with a hefty price. He not only gave her the gift of youth and beauty but that of black magic, true witchcraft. She had powers that could not be matched by any mere mortal. With her hands, she could deliver death to the living. She was now a creature of darkness. She performed the dark master's bidding as she sought out her revenge.

When you came too close to her, you smelled the decay of her rotting flesh. She was rumored to attack people in their bed as they slept. She pinned down her victim, preventing them from moving. They were unable to scream, unable to escape from her deadly grasp. Once she had you in her grips she stole your dreams, leaving you forever with griping nightmares. While under her spell, she marred your perfect beauty by leaving you with whip marks as evidence of her attack.

She lived in an old shack which sat atop rotting timbers. Loud grunts from her creatures sounded out along the banks, as water lapped against the pier.

In this place dwelt only darkness, she kept her home hidden by trickery and magic. A monstrous expanse of trees guarded her home and announced danger to those who entered.

Soon after she moved into the tiny shack the green vegetation shriveled and died. Light only dared to touch this area for a few hours each day. Wherever her evil touched, it left in its wake devastation.

On the outskirts of her swamp was a tiny Cajun village, filled with elderly women. Not a man or child could be found in this sad village. They warned any who ventured this way of the witch's powers. The witch that lived in the swamp was true evil and must be feared, for they knew of her power.

Behind their village was a veil of mists where darkness dwelled. The creatures that lived there were no longer that of their former selves, but strange evil creatures cursed by the witch herself.

The swamp was surrounded by an eerie thick fog that oozed from rotting stumps. Everywhere the witch walked, she left behind death and destruction. The swamp was nothing more than a mere shadow of what it once was.

Sounds of the nightmarish creatures that lurked in the slimy muck echoed through the night. Demonic dragon-like creatures roosted on Cypress Knees protruding from the water and waited for the next poor soul to wander their way.

Plants here coiled around your legs, forbidding you the chance to escape. The quicksand could swallow a person whole. A rustle echoed through the swamp as snakes and other slithering creatures scurried to move out of death's way.

***

The wind rushed through the trees as the barefoot woman walked through the muck. The animals here feared her powers, knowing that with the wave of her hand they could cease to exist. Off in the distance she heard an air boat moving through the foggy swamp. She anxiously waited to see if her creatures brought her back another treat.

She despised the tales that have been passed along for others to share, *"A witch lies in the woods, waiting for a maiden to fall fast asleep. That is when she comes, in their dreams, dragging them deep into nightmares of which they will not return."*

Those who have dared to find their way to her swamp became servants of the Nightmare Witch. As another creature fell under her spell, she knew once more that there was no end to her power.

Over the years tales had been told, warning of the monsters that lived in the swamps. They told of hunters who ventured deep into the swamps only never to return. They were forever cursed as the devil's servants.

The tales told of a beautiful woman who lived out in the swamps. Her beauty was so tempting, that whenever a man saw her he was cursed, turned into a fearful beast.

The Cajuns nearby feared her so much that on a full moon no male dared leave his door unlocked. The windows were barred up tight and the shutters closed. Young maids were not permitted to sleep that night in fear that the Nightmare Witch would find them in their dreams.

***

From the glass jar she drew a long pinch of the white powder and sprinkled it evenly over the potion bubbling in the cauldron hanging over a blue flame. Tonight was a full moon, the perfect time to concoct this potion. The small trapped animal inside the cage sensed something afoot and stirred restlessly.

She perused the dark charms, morbid objects, and various decanters in search of the next ingredient. Removing a small bottle, she dropped a tiny amount into the potion and watched as it diffused into a blood red cloud. Once again, she searched the shelves until she found her next ingredient. A frown formed on her face when she realized her supply was almost exhausted from the many years of careful use. The next crescent moon she needed to gather ingredients once again.

Adding a small dash of the final ingredient, the potion clarified. She let the potion simmer for a few more minutes before hovering her hand over the cauldron's contents. Reciting the incantation, the brew turned from a glowing red to a vibrant yellow. The flames in the hearth began to rise, forming a hollow mouth and eyes. As the image continued to grow in size, the smoke of the flames gathered to take shape. Eyes formed in the sunken sockets. A thousand voices rushed through the hollow mouth. The image vanished once the incantation was finished.

Her lips parted in a menacing smile. She has performed this secret incantation over and over for many years. She stroked the edge of the cauldron with a well-manicured pale finger.

She brought a spoonful of the liquid over to the small rabbit. "Come now, my pet. You must only drink but a sip." Her voice remained low and vibrating.

As the rabbit transformed into a tiny red hobgoblin, known as a Nain Rouge, she felt her powers strengthening once more.

As she moved about the room, her bones began to ache. Soon she would need the soul of an innocent. Just being in their presence she could taste their sweet innocence. Her lips would feed off of it before they even had a chance to scream. Their withered bodies would be hidden deep in the tiny village she had constructed for them. Their bodies were nothing but a shell after she stripped them of their youthfulness.

As if sensing what his mistress desired, a Rougarou brought in a young girl. She looked at her with disgust showing in her eyes, "This..." Pointing to the girl she spat out, "This is the best that you could find."

Without waiting any further, she seized the child and drained her of her life force. Dropping the withered body onto the ground without remorse, she hissed, "You must make better selections for me. Definitely something more than what you brought me."

The Rougarou watched as his mistress's cheeks grew tighter, the darkened spots on her skin receded, and her hands less gnarled with age.

With a tremor in his body, he nodded his understanding. "Their beauty must be exquisite. She must be a perfect little innocent, so full of promise." She explained once again.

Wishing to please his mistress, he cringed at the mere thought of disappointing her again. Truly innocent girls were difficult to come by as of late. They must seek out younger girls if they wanted one that innocent. If he did find one who had beauty beyond reproach he would be rewarded handsomely.

Looking down at the creature, she ordered, "Why are you still here? Go! Get out of my sight. Do not return until you have one that is worthy of me." Kicking the body of the girl, she said, "Go and take this with you. Do with it what you will. I have no need for it."

She watched as the Rougarou vanished in a puff of smoke. Why was it so hard for these creatures to find her girls so pure of heart? Surely there must be a few living in the neighboring towns. If only she had known that everlasting beauty meant she must repeat the spell for eternity. Fate had played a cruel trick on her.

Chapter 3

Blackwater Bayou, Louisiana 1955

The Nightmare Witch's breakfast this morning consisted of the hearts from six pretty cardinals, the bright red a stark contrast to the darkness that surrounded her. She plunged her index finger deep into the tiny bodies and plucked out the heart. The organ was no bigger than a pea which she swallowed in one bite, letting the sweet blood trickle down her throat.

Even after one hundred years her skin remained taut and flawless. Not a line marred her face. In fact, she looked even younger than when she was granted immortality. She became more beautiful with each passing year.

She looked outside at the world she had created for herself. All around her were things that she had taken. That was what made her happy, when she stole the dreams from the beautiful and left behind nothing but a nightmare. When she stole the beauty of the woodland creatures and left behind a grotesque form.

Revenge consumed her. Revenge twisted inside of her, deep in the very center of her being. Venom dripped from her pores.

Tonight was the perfect night for magie noire, black magic. Tonight, magie noire would prevail as it consumed this place. This was a night of strange beginnings, or endings.

As the young man hunted in the swamp, a vile creature, standing just over five feet tall and covered with fine hair, appeared. It had cloven hooves for feet and a short tail of a goat. Even the head of the creature resembled a goat more than a man, complete with a small pair of horns protruding from the top of its head. A large pair of red eyes glowed in the dark as it moved closer to him. Suddenly the creature let out an ear piercing scream as it revealed a set of long, sharp fangs dripping with blood. The creature quickly captured the young hunter and brought him to its mistress.

She greeted the creature, "Welcome, my pet, you have done well tonight." She turned to the young hunter and explained, "This is one of my latest creations. It is a Grunch, half-man and half-goat. He and a few of his brothers protect the perimeters of my land." She ran a finger along the hunter's strong jaw line. "But you, mon cher, are to join my Rougarou." From the darkness, even more creatures arrived. These creatures had the shape of half-wolf and half-man. With a sinister smile, she taunted him, "These will be your brothers." She looked over at the Rougarou forming a circle around them. "Welcome your new brother, my loves."

With a sinister laugh, the Nightmare Witch informed the young man, "I have the Dukes of Hell and alchemists to thank for my powers and, of course, my pets." She stretched languidly in the moonlight and explained, "The Dukes of Hell gave me what I desired most you see — immortality." Taking one of the cardinals from the cage, she used a long fingernail to cut open its chest, and removed its still beating heart. She swallowed it in one gulp.

As she chanted, a piercing cold spread throughout him. The chanting slowly increased and rose in tempo. His skin melted off and was replaced with fur. He screamed out in agony as his body was transformed into the hideous Rougarou.

Chapter 4
1965

When the Nightmare Witch walked out to her garden early in the morning, the sun had yet to rise. She wanted to gather some of her prized herbs that she needed for her spells. She gathered only what she needed because she refused to harvest the entire plant, needing the original for seeds.

She wanted to make a few creatures even more evil than her pet Rougarou. Tonight would be the perfect night for her newest experiment.

After she had added the ingredients from her garden into the cauldron, she reached up, grabbed her jar of dead man's toes, and added one of the fouler smelling ones to the potion.

Next she added the last ingredient from the tiny pouch that hung from the belt at her waist, graveyard dust. She sprinkled the dust over the potion and watched as it diffused into a deep green haze.

After the potion clarified, she recited her incantation. The brew turned from a glowing green to a vibrant red. An image formed out of the flames and smoke. Once the incantation was finished, everything vanished.

Chapter 5
1990

Hidden in the thick swamp vegetation the creature surreptitiously watched as the men stealthily paddled the small boat through the stagnant water. They had long ago cut the boat's noisy motor and trimmed the engine to where it was no longer in the water. The oars made virtually no sound as they pushed against the water.

With the sun directly up above them, the heat radiated off of the water. An occasional shrill of a bird would break the silence as a random breeze ruffled the tops of the tall trees. Out on the water, the air was hot, sticky, and damp from the humidity of the day.

The creature's footsteps remained silent as it walked to the edge of the water. The creature heard one of the men say, "Dere should be plenty of big alligators out dis way."

His partner shook his head and replied, "Mais, I hope ya are right 'bout dis. I still don't know why ya wanted to come out dis way. Dis is too close to da old witch's cabin."

Laughing the first man said, "Ya worry too much, mon ami. Mais, no one ventures out dis far. De alligators should be plentiful out here." Looking out over the water, he explained, "Besides, dose are just stories da old folks like to tell. Dere is no witch dat lives out dere."

Suddenly a thick fog moved over the swamp, covering everything as far as the eye could see. The two men had to squint to make out anything.

Unbeknownst to the men, the creature slipped into the water and glided towards the boat. As the boat began to rock in the murky bayou water, the men's hearts pounded ferociously in their chest. "Mon ami, something tells me dat we need to head back da other way and get outta here."

As the boat continued to rock, his friend agreed, "Dis fog will probably be gone as we move closer to da dock."

As they dropped the oars into the water, a strange looking creature pulled itself onto the boat. However, instead of pulling itself all the way into the boat it pushed the men towards the bank. "Harold, hurry up and choot it."

Harold aimed his gun straight at the center of the creature's chest and fired. They watched in horrified silence as the bullets bounced off of the creature instead of killing it. Harold exclaimed, "I know dat I hit the beast, but it didn't die."

As the boat hit the bank of the bayou with a soft thud, the men suddenly found themselves surrounded by even more horrifying creatures. As the oversized wolf-like creatures glared at them with their amber glowing eyes, both men had to swallow down the fear overcoming their bodies.

With their sharp fangs exposed, the growling creatures sprang on the men, dragging them from the boat.

As they moved even deeper into the swamp, they heard the loud thumping beat of drums followed by a softer tat-a -tat-tat. The pulse had a steady hypnotizing rhythm. The swamp came alive as each tree and shrub nearby swayed in beat to the throbbing rhythm. The noise overpowered the high-pitched womanlike scream of a minx as it scurried off into the underbrush.

The path meandered its way through the murky swamp. The area here was as black as the spirits which dwelled there. The beat sounded as if it was coming from all directions.

The full moon illuminated the ritual site. The Rougarou carefully laid the men down amidst a circle of candles and skulls. As the Nain Rouge lit torches, they tried to take in what was happening. This had to be a nightmare.

A woman appeared and two more Nain Rouge emerged from the shadows, carrying a brazier that bellowed forth sweet smelling lavender tinted smoke. They placed the brazier in front of the men as the sweet vapors wafted about.

***

The Nightmare Witch arranged two wooden bowls on the altar, one filled with murky swamp water and the other with alligator blood. She placed a dagger made of bone and a book bound in human flesh on the altar.

She leafed through the book, searching for a specific page. She turned to face the men in the center of the circle as the creatures chanted. As they chanted, their feet rose and fell to the beat of the drums, rising and falling with the staccato. The Nightmare Witch picked up the dagger and cut a lock of each man's hair. She took the hair, placed some in the bowl of blood and some in the bowl of water. As she joined in the chant, her voice rang out over the others. She picked up the bowl of blood and poured the contents over their heads. As she raised her arms, their bodies elevated off the ground. A deep guttural moan escaped their mouths as her eyes turned black as night.

The chanting rose to a feverish pitch. The ground vibrated as the creatures moved in closer.

One of the men screamed out in terror as the woman's face contorted into a demonic appearance. Over and over she continued to chant. As the music, dancing, and chanting reached a crescendo, the men let out a piercing scream that tore through the night air. Their bodies went into convulsions, twisting to and fro in mid-air. One of the men began violently frothing at the mouth as he thrashed about.

When they fell to the ground, the Nightmare Witch smiled. "Stand," she ordered. The creatures stood in front of her, snapping at the creatures surrounding them. "You must not harm your brothers, my children. Now, go to the swamp and protect my waters."

With a nod of their heads, the creatures dropped to the ground and crawled back into the murky swamp waters from which they were born. The Nightmare Witch was proud of her latest creatures. She would have to make more of these alligator men. They could prove to be very useful, perhaps even more so than her Rougarou.

As she watched her creatures glide into the water, a bullfrog jumped up onto the bank. She opened her poison ring and sprinkled it with the powder contained within. Its tiny body shook as a new form emerged; another Nain Rouge appeared before her.

The agony of those she cursed could sometimes be heard in the quietness of the night. Their moans carried with the wind.

The Nightmare Witch was pleased with herself. Every day she waited for another being to wander into her swamp. With her demonic powers, she transformed living creatures into her own small evil army.

Her creatures constantly sought out new animals that wandered near. They must wait for her permission before they devoured any they found, in case she wanted it for her army. Once permission was given their sharp, fang-like teeth pierced the animal's body, causing it immediate death.

Her greatest joy was when a hunter wandered into her swamp, but these were few and far between lately. The Nightmare Witch cursed the Cajun village at the edge of her land. Had she not been generous enough to allow them to live? And this was how they treated her, by warning others of her.

Suddenly one of her creatures cried out, alerting her that a stranger was nearby. She ordered them, "Bring him to me alive."

***

Strange dragon-like birds called out from up above; their guttural shrieks sent shivers down his back as he wandered deeper into this strange area of the swamp. Terrible noises echoed all around him as he swallowed back his fear. He must turn around; this was not the way home.

The ground was soggy beneath his feet. The moss hanging in the trees seemed to reach out for him. Suddenly the shape of a creature appeared in front of him. He bit back a scream as he saw the creature was well over six feet tall, built like a man but had the appearance of a wolf.

Fearing what this creature had planned for him, he took off in a run. He pushed his body to move faster as his breath became ragged and hoarse.

The terrain was rough around him. His foot caught on a giant tree root that sent him hurtling through the air. He landed with a thud amongst a patch of black mushrooms. A sticky green cloud of pollen escaped from them and settled on his body.

His vision blurred as the trees took on a strange form around him. Hooded figures, menacing and black, emerged from the shadows, waiting to capture him.

Giant roots wrapped around his body, and taunted him, "Look what we have here, a stranger."

The Rougarou called out from the shadows, "She wants him brought to her unharmed."

The giant roots and black forms slunk back into the trees, not wanting to upset their master. As the creatures moved in closer to him, his mind plunged into a blackened abyss from which there was no escape. Dark, velvety oblivion welcomed him with open arms.

***

She paced her small shack until her Rougarou arrived with the young man in tow, "Why did you wander into these woods? Did you not hear about what lives here?"

He could barely speak, but answered, "I am lost and could not find my way back to town."

One of her Rougarou stepped forward, asking, "May we please have this one for our food? Our teeth are sharp and ready. We are desperate for the taste of human blood."

"No!" she exclaimed.

While looking at the handsome man in front of her, she reached into the bowl of cardinals in front of her and plucked out a tasty heart. She enjoyed the gentle give of the meat as she contemplated what to do with this man.

Neither of them spoke as he stared at her, eyes ablaze from within. She grabbed his face and stared deep into his deep blue eyes.

Looking at his handsome face, rage built inside of her, the fury mixing with her blood. "You, mon cher, like to break young girls' hearts. How would you like to know how it feels?" She hissed in his ear.

She moved her hand to his chest, and hovered just over his shirt, but never touched him. She paralyzed him with her magic. The beat of his heart echoed in her ears. It grew louder with each passing second.

She allowed the magic to consume her, sweeping her away with its raging current. *How dare such a beautiful man enter her lands!* She leaned back as the power filled her fingertips, speeding up his heartbeat.

She willed his heart to beat faster; it obeyed. She repeated once more FASTER! Once again, it obeyed. Each beat blended into the next, the sound echoing in the small room.

The man's eyes became frantic. They were bulging and red. The Nightmare Witch centered her strength and forced her hand deep into his chest, encircling it around his heart. She gripped her fist tighter and tighter as he grimaced in pain.

The pounding of his heart filled her ears until his heart ceased to beat. The man slumped to the ground in a heap as she fell backwards, landing heavy against the nearby wall.

She could barely stand as her body stooped forward. This little parlor trick had taken more energy than she should have used. Why must her power come at a hefty price? She already felt the small wrinkles forming on her face and feared to look in the mirror.

As her skin grew paper thin, she knew that the expense of what she just did had cost her more than she was ready to give. Looking at her pets, she ordered, "Leave the body for now. Whoever brings me an innocent, untouched child will get to devour the body for themselves." She knew that, for now, she was too weak to enter into a young girl's dreams, and would instead need a flesh and blood child.

The Rougarou took off at once, fighting amongst themselves as to who would be the first out of the small shack.

By the time they had returned, she barely had the energy to stand.

A young girl was dropped to her feet, possibly sixteen years old. She tried to move far away from the creatures in front of her.

The Nightmare Witch ordered the Rougarou, "Lift her for me."

She looked over at the girl who had been brought to her. She took in the stunning caramel color of her skin, raven black hair, and dark as coffee eyes. "You have done well my pet."

The Nightmare Witch smiled at the innocent child, enjoying everything about this one. She ran her finger along the girl's face, "She is perfect."

The young girl squirmed in the Rougarou's firm grasp, "Please let me go." She twisted and turned, trying to free herself as The Nightmare Witch stepped forward. "What... What are you going to do to me," she quietly asked.

A smile formed across the Nightmare Witch's face as she brought her hand to the girl's neck and closed her fingers tightly around her throat. The young girl opened her mouth to scream, but no sound came out. The witch's pale lips twisted into a vicious grin. Her eyes sparkled with glitters of black.

The very essence of the girl's youth threatened to pour out of her. Her aura was one of sweet innocence.

She tilted her head back and let the girl's energy flow from her body into her very being. She drank in the goodness and purity that flowed through her. The girl's heart pounded fiercely as she drank in her life force. It filled her from her toes to the top of her head, restoring her beauty. She felt the skin on her body tighten as her youth was restored.

She dropped her to the floor as a renewed power once more pulsed through her body.

The Rougarou swarmed in front of the young girl. Her youth was no longer apparent. Her body was now gnarled. Her skin withered and wrinkled, her hair wiry and snow white. She looked to be nearly eighty years old with all traces of her beauty gone.

The witch felt no remorse for what she did to the girl. She felt her powers strengthening.

She addressed the Rougarou who brought her the lovely young girl, "Now you can have your reward." Throwing the girl to the ground, she instructed him, "But first, drop her off at the village."

Picking up the semi-unconscious girl as if she weighed nothing, the Rougarou dragged the man's body behind him. He would bring the body to the swamp to enjoy his well-deserved meal.

***

The sounds of the night drifted into the tiny room from the open window. Bullfrogs croaked out love songs in hopes of finding a mate, a snake hissed into the wind as it searched for a meal, and the leaves rustled as the wind blew through the trees.

Suddenly everything fell quiet. Rose bolted awake as the soothing night sounds ceased. She grabbed her shawl from the rocking chair next to her bed and wrapped it tight around her shoulders. As she brewed a pot of tea, she looked out her kitchen window. The moon was full, and a thin ribbon of fog snaked through the trees surrounding the back of her yard.

She stared into the fog moving in and waited for what was to come. Soon the sound of terrifying screams filled the night. A shiver ran through her as she imagined what all this poor soul must be enduring right now. Soon the swamp around her would be filled with another of the Nightmare Witch's evil creations.

Chapter 6

Kingston, New York March 2005

The Nightmare Witch stood at the side of the road and watched, waiting for her prey. She had her hair haphazardly bundled on top of her head, pinned in place with several of her prized bone combs. Her long skirt blew in the breeze as she stared out into the night. The vegetation around her shivered in fear as she continued to wait. If only the blasted woman had not cast a spell to prevent the Nightmare Witch from harming her in her dreams or those of her newborn daughter. One of these days, though, her powers would be strong enough to counter any spell these witches could cast. Then no one could stop her.

Her prey would be here soon; she could feel it in her bones. These last few days she has come to learn the woman's every move. She has sensed her growing fear, and worse, the child's growing powers. She has seen it in the cards; this child must be vanquished from this earth. This mere child has it inside of herself to send her back to the fires of Hell. That must never come to fruition. No, she refused to give up this life she has made for herself in this mortal realm.

As the headlights of the car came closer, she prepared to make her move. Although she could have done this from the comfort of her home, she preferred to see the devastation in person. Raising her hands, with the flick of her wrist she sent the car careening through the air. The sound of screeching metal and glass shattering broke the silence of the peaceful night.

***

As Carla Bradford felt the life leaving her body, she realized the fatal mistake that she has made. She had been foolish to think that she could stop her daughter's destiny. She never wanted a life of magic for her newborn child, and now she was leaving her daughter unprotected in a world full of danger. If only she had told Ted that she was a witch, and so was their daughter. Instead, she had renounced her family and anything involving magic.

She should have listened to her Aunt Helen's warnings, but she had been foolish and believed she could keep her child protected.

Chapter 7

Blackwater Bayou, Louisiana May 2014

"There it is Lizzy." Her dad slowed down the moving truck and pointed to the large house, wait, no he said it was called a plantation. "That is our new home thanks to an elderly great aunt of yours."

Lizzy wished she had a better view of the home, but the trees were in the way. If only the wind would blow. She waved her hand in the air, as if the simple movement would do as she wished. Her breath caught when coincidentally the wind did blow, swaying the tree limbs just enough for her to get a glimpse of her future home.

Lizzy just stared at the large house in disbelief. She still didn't understand how all of this came about. When her dad told her about the strange letter and her inheritance, it had sounded too good to be true. And now, here she was staring at their new house. No more tiny apartment, no more rules about pets. "And I can have a puppy Daddy?"

Ted Bradford smiled over at his precocious ten year old daughter, "You can have a puppy, a kitten, or a whole farm. I don't care. I just want to see you smile." Ted reminded her, "This will be a big change for us. There are no noisy neighbors; well actually there aren't any neighbors at all. You won't have any friends to run off and play with. It will be just you and me in this large house, all to ourselves."

As they made their way down the drive, birds flew out of the trees, surprised by the arrival of a visitor. The driveway was horseshoe shaped with old oak trees flanking both sides of the house. A large porch wrapped around the whole house, on both the first and second floor. Enormous columns helped to hold up the porches along with a breathtaking twin staircase that went from the ground to the second story, both swooping outward in the opposite direction from the middle.

To no one in particular, he stated, "Can you imagine what it took to build this house back then?"

Now that the truck was stopped Lizzy took off her seatbelt and threw her arms around her daddy, "I love the house. There are so many rooms that I can explore and I will have friends when I go to school." Opening her door, she called out to her dad, "Come on, Daddy. I want to see what the inside looks like."

As Ted looked around, he realized that the house was in better shape than he had suspected. He never even knew that his wife, Carla, had relatives here in Louisiana much less one that knew of his daughter's birth.

Before opening the door, he told her, "If you do not like it here then we can always sell the house and move somewhere else."

"Oh no, Daddy. Hurry up and open the door. I can't wait to see the inside."

As they walked in, Lizzy cried out, "Oh Daddy, isn't it just beautiful. I have never seen anything like this." As she ran down the hall, she called out, "Do you think mom would have loved this place?"

Ted felt the sadness grip his heart, "I am sure of it honey. She always loved to go antique shopping and even adventures. I bet if she were here right now she could tell us what period each piece of furniture was from."

As Ted looked around, he envisioned Carla dancing around this house in excitement. She would have wanted to explore every nook and cranny, inspect each piece of furniture. The house was full of antiques, and from the looks of it, valuable items. There was furniture, vases, and even some statues.

Lizzy loved hearing stories about her mother. She has only seen photos of the woman who gave her life. She died when Lizzy was a baby, but she missed her just the same. Lately, she has been having more dreams about her mother sitting on the edge of her bed and talking to her.

As Lizzy moved around the massive downstairs of the house, she stopped in front of a picture hanging over the fireplace. "Dad, do you think this is the great aunt who left us the house?"

Ted looked at the picture and was surprised to see such a stark resemblance to his wife in the picture, "She could be. Your mother looked a lot like her."

Filled with excitement now Lizzy exclaimed, "I sure hope there are more pictures here for us to see."

After exploring the house for a little longer they began to make trip after trip to the moving van. There was luggage, groceries, and other personal items that needed to be unloaded first. Ted told Lizzy, "We may as well leave the rest of the stuff for now. Tomorrow we can unload it."

Looking around once more, he said, "I am not even sure where to put our furniture."

By nine o'clock that night both father and daughter were tired. Lizzy leapt into bed and pulled the covers tight over her as her dad checked the room once more. "Good night honey. Sleep tight and don't let the bed bugs bite."

Giggling, she answered, "Daddy, you are so silly." Reaching up she gave him a kiss on his cheek before settling down in the bed once more.

Outside, she heard the wind rustling the leaves of the large oak. The moon cast eerie shadows that danced around her room. The strange night sounds of the new house kept her from falling asleep. With each new creak, she wondered what had made the noise. She tossed and turned, flipping to the right, then the left, on her back, and then on her stomach. However, no matter which position she tried she couldn't shut out the noises or get comfortable.

After what felt like hours, she drifted off into a deep sleep. She had the strangest dream. She found herself alone in a dark forest, almost devoid of life. Tall, black trees loomed over her. There was no movement or sound yet she sensed something in the dark, watching her. Fearfully she slowly looked around, but saw nothing. She walked deeper into the forest, unsure of which direction she was going. She jumped back as the moss from the trees appeared to reach for her. The damp ground under her feet caused her to sink deeper into the wet floor. With each step the smell of decaying leaves filled the air. A noise behind her caught her attention and she tried to run, but the wet ground hindered her movements.

An eerie light out of nowhere filled the night sky. A woman wearing a cloak stepped from a cloud of green smoke. The hair that hung down from the hood cascaded down her body in long tendrils, twisting and twining like long black snakes. She held a staff made from ancient black jack vines, topped with a crystal that shimmered in the moonlight in her left hand. She stretched out a bony hand towards Lizzy. Lizzy let out a gasp when she saw the woman's skin was as pale as a ghost. Even though Lizzy could not see her eyes she felt them on her, burning her skin like acid. As the woman took a step closer to Lizzy, she instinctively stepped back.

Her heart pounded fiercely in her chest. Her breath came out in nothing more than slow, shallow bursts. She has never been so afraid.

The woman did not speak. Instead, she slowly walked towards Lizzy. The woman's vile scent seemed to fill Lizzy's mind as she made her way closer.

The hatred this woman felt for Lizzy radiated from her very being. Lizzy could not explain why the woman hated her so, as she had never seen her before, but there was no denying the hatred this woman felt for her.

***

Hidden in the shadows of the swamp she watched the father and child move into the house. They laughed and chatted as they unloaded the large van. The girl's honey brown hair shimmered in the sunlight. She caught sight of the young girl's face and noticed her beauty. She would break all kinds of hearts growing up.

Pangs of jealousy swirled deep inside of her. She would visit the girl tonight in her dreams, taunt her. Soon she would know just how powerful of a witch she was. This girl was the last of the LeDoux blood line, the last of those who could vanquish her from this earth.

Each day that this girl lived, the Nightmare Witch felt the girl's powers growing stronger. They were rapidly gaining strength now that she was here. She must be eradicated before her powers had a chance to fully manifest.

Rage flowed through the witch as the child smiled happily up at her father. She wished she could rip their hearts out at this very moment, but soon, soon she would bring them sorrow. Soon the father would have a fierce ache deep in his heart. His breath would catch just at the mere thought of his missing daughter. He would have sleepless nights as he wondered where she had gone to.

Chapter 8

The following night as Lizzy was nestled comfortably in her bed, dreaming peacefully, she heard the frightening howls of what resembled a wolf slice through the silence like a high pitched wail in the wind. Piercing and shrill, the howls stirred her from her sleep.   She lifted her head, rubbed her tired eyes groggily and slowly opened them. Her room was nothing but a blur, as were her thoughts. Sleep called her back to its warm embrace, and listening to it, she closed her eyes once more.

She would rather return to her dream instead of leaving the comforts of her bed to find out just what was howling outside her window. As she drifted off to sleep the howling started once again. She laughed at how silly her fear was. There were no wolves here in Louisiana but as the howl carried through the night once more, a shiver of fear snaked up her spine. She wrapped her arms around her tiny body and held her breath. The howls sounded as if they were very near to the house. Fear chased away her drowsiness.

She eased herself out of bed and crossed the room on unsteady legs. Concealed by her curtains, she peeked out behind the pane into the night. The full moon cast a gentle glow on the yard. The landscape was a picturesque scene of serenity. She opened her window a little more and listened to the night.

Once again, an eerie howl sounded through the night. She wondered what kind of creature would make that noise. As the wails rose, she realized how close the creature was to her house. The howls became so menacing that she closed her bedroom window, fearing that they could come into her room.

As the noises continued, she took it as a clear warning for her to stay out of the swamp, especially at night. Yet, she knew that she would not be able to heed their warning. She has been anxiously waiting to explore the swamp.

As another howl sounded, curiosity overcame her. She searched through the boxes in her bedroom, looking for the binoculars. She gazed into the night in hopes of seeing movement.

The weeping willow branches blew gracefully in the night breeze. A deer darted through the edge of the woods. Was the deer running from whatever was howling? Then her breath caught in her throat. She zoomed in, certain that she had imagined what she saw. Yet, the glowing red eyes were there at the edge of the swamp. She stepped back in fear. It appeared as if the eyes were staring right at her.

After climbing back into bed, it took Lizzy a good long time to fall asleep. The next morning, once she finished eating her breakfast, she went exploring. As soon as she stepped outside, the humid air stuck to her. It surprised her that it was so hot down here, even this early in the morning.

As she walked deeper into the swamp, she noticed that the foliage here was so thick that the sun could barely peek through. The briar bushes and underbrush scratched her legs as she searched for the spot where she saw the glowing red eyes. Turning back towards the house, she located her bedroom window. She soon found the spot where she saw the eyes and was surprised to discover a narrow, windy path.

She listened to the animals in the swamp, fearing that she may hear the wolf again in the daylight. A bird shrilled deep in the forest as a woodpecker hammered on a tree nearby. She listened as the crickets and other insects sang their songs as well, welcoming a new day. Leaves rustled in the gentle breeze as the trees swayed. She took in a deep breath of the fresh air. It was thick and cloying, with a tangy scent of pine needles. She could even smell the rich, damp earth.

Swatting at the tiny gnats that found her attractive, she walked deeper into the woods. The ground became wetter further from the house. The gnats became even thicker further into the swamp. Her arms itched just at the thought of the pesky insects.   Out of nowhere, something up ahead scampered behind a fallen log.

Deciding that she had enough adventure for now, she turned back. It didn't take her long to realize that she was lost. The sound of water caught her attention. Maybe if she followed the bayou that ran along the property she could find her way back home. She should have brought her cell phone with her, but as usual she forgot to make sure that it was charged.

As she made her way to the water's edge, she gasped. The water here was dark and murky. It appeared thicker than the water near the house. Now and then it let out a disgusting gurgle as it churned. With each air bubble that formed and popped, a foul smell was emitted.

Two shadows formed on the water from up above. Shielding her eyes as she looked up in the sky, Lizzy watched two large birds circle above her. They had to be some of the largest buzzards she has ever seen. Her dad said that when buzzards circled they were telling others that they found food, which meant they found something dead. A shiver of fear ran through Lizzy. The last thing she wanted was to stumble on a dead animal that other animals were eating.

Lizzy continued following the water, hoping that she was heading in the right direction to her house. After several minutes, she stopped under the deep shade of a tree to catch her breath before continuing. By this time, she was really sweating.

What she wouldn't give for a breeze right now. The air in the swamp was heavy, and nothing seemed to be moving here.

Out of nowhere a loud cawing from up above caught her attention. The buzzards that she had spotted earlier were right above her. The enormous birds seemed to be peering down at her. She watched as they settled on a dead branch of a tree. For the first time Lizzy noticed her surroundings. She had indeed gone in the wrong direction. Nothing here looked familiar. In fact, this particular area of the swamp has an eerie feeling to it. There were no longer any lush trees or underbrush; everything was black and gloomy.

Letting out a loud moan, the birds cawed once more before taking flight. They soared away as Lizzy felt tears building up inside of her.

As her heart pounded hard in her chest, and panic rose high in her body, she forced herself to look around. Something had to look familiar here. But it didn't. She was completely and utterly lost. At least this time she had been following the water so all she had to do was turn around and head back the other way.

As Lizzy headed back, she stopped and rubbed her eyes. She could have sworn that the roots of the large tree moved. She screamed as something slithered up her ankle. Suddenly she found herself falling fast to the ground. As she landed on her knees, her heart pounded hard in her chest.

She was too afraid to find out what had grabbed her ankle. She sighed with relief when she saw that she had only tripped on a tree root sticking out of the ground. All around her were upraised tree roots that reminded her of large snakes frozen in time.

She frantically scrambled up from the tangle of roots and mud. Up ahead, for the first time since venturing into this area, she heard an animal scurrying about. Out of curiosity, she went to see which animal it was. She wanted to find a little bunny to take home and raise as a pet. As she pushed through the briar patch disappointment filled her. Whatever had been here must have hurried off.

The swamp here was still dead, but at least there seemed to be more vegetation. There were mushrooms growing on the base of the trees. Some were as black as night and as large as a football while others were gray and the size of a quarter. For a moment she thought the mushrooms actually disappeared into the ground as if afraid of being picked.

Past the mushrooms and trees, she stared in shocked surprise at the tiny shack on the edge of the bayou waters. The dilapidated building sat perched haphazardly on long stilts as if it was waiting for a gust of wind to send it crashing into the water.

Lizzy wondered what treasures the old house must hold. She imagined that at one time it might have been a playhouse for one of the children who must have lived on this plantation. Maybe they left behind old toys that were valuable now.

Letting her imagination go even further, she started to believe that this was the shack where a witch lived. Perhaps her spell books were in there waiting for Lizzy to find. As she walked closer, she noticed that it was much older than she first thought. The thatched roof consisted of branches and grass. The walls were old pieces of wood haphazardly slapped together. The door was tree limbs bound together. There were no windows to be seen. How depressing it must be to live in a place that didn't allow any light in. Surely no one could live in such an old shack, especially in such a depressing area of the swamp.

A little voice told her that whoever was living here wanted to stay hidden. They didn't want the world to know that they lived here. She stopped and looked once more. Something deep inside of her warned her to go home, to run as quick as she could. That someone evil lived in the tiny shack.

This time Lizzy listened to her gut and ran in the other direction. She ran over the rough terrain, not caring that the briars scratched her legs or that her feet sank deeper into the mud with each step. She had to get out of here, she must get home.

Gasping for air, she ran even faster. Sharp vines and dense leaves slapped at her face and arms. She continued on, fearing if she stopped something would grab her.

The scenery around her became a blur of light and shade, trees, and vines. She ran through the swamp as fast as she could. Something grabbed at her ankles, knocking her to the ground hard. Rocks and branches cut painfully through her clothes. Her skin burned with each cut. Tears rushed to her eyes. She reached out defensively for whatever had her ankles, but was greeted with nothing but cold air. Above her, she saw interwoven branches of tall trees watching her.

Pushing herself off the ground, she didn't bother to look for what could be behind her. Instead, she focused on getting home. Sprinting out of the thick woods at the edge of the swamp, she was relieved to see the path that led back to her house. She didn't even bother to look back at the strange trees lining the area she had just fled. She didn't notice the thicket of dark roots that seemed to reach out for her in hopes of dragging her back to the dark swamp. Instead, she continued running. Her chest heaved, her throat was dry, and a sharp pain penetrated her right side. She pushed on, not wanting to look back.

In the distance she saw the plantation. She paused to catch her breath. She finally made it back home.

Once inside, Lizzy quickly locked the door. She didn't think
she could have run any further. She was out of breath, her
legs burned, and her heart was pumping so hard her chest
ached with exertion. She felt like jelly all over. Leaning
over, she braced her hands on her knees, trying to catch her
breath.

Her dad called out, "I was worried about you. I thought you
had gotten lost."

Nodding her head as she gasped for air, she told him, "I was
lost. I got turned around in the swamp." Drawing another
breath, she added, "Dad, the swamp is dying in the back.
There is a shack on the bayou. It looks really old."

"Hmm, well it sounds like you had quite an adventure
then." Giving his daughter a stern look he said, "I don't
want you venturing so far out without letting me know."

Hugging her father, glad to see him, she replied, "Don't
worry, Daddy. I have no plans on going into the swamps
anymore. That place is scary and I learned that it is super
easy to get lost back there."

Later that night Lizzy and her dad went for another walk.
She felt more comfortable walking in the swamp with him
by her side.

They watched as the sky darkened. It went from a bright
blue to a blaze of fiery reds and deep oranges. Slowly the
deep purple of night moved in. From the courtyard out
back, Lizzy watched the full moon. She didn't think the
moon or stars were ever this bright in the city.

As she settled back into bed, the strange, frightening howls began once more. As she fell into a deep sleep, the unsettling dreams started again. She was back in the swamp, but this time something was chasing her. As she picked up her speed the howling wolves surrounded her, their red eyes watched her intently. She found herself in the eerie part of the swamp. The howling wolves were now behind her, chasing her. Too afraid to look back, she ran faster, praying that she was running in the right direction. Without warning, her feet stop moving. Looking down, she discovered she was standing in quicksand. She thrashed about, trying to free herself. In the next instant, she was surrounded by glowing red eyes.

Bolting upright in bed, it took Lizzy a moment to calm her racing heart. She eased out of the bed, double and triple checking the bedroom window to make sure it was locked. In the darkness of the night, the unrelenting howling continued. A shiver of fear snaked up her spine. Tonight she was too afraid to peek out the window, fearing that she would see the glowing red eyes looking into her bedroom once more.

A piercing howl bounced off her room walls. It sounded as if it came from right outside her window this time. Swallowing down her fear, she peeked outside the window, gently moving the curtains back. The full moon cast a ghostly pallor over the yard. She scanned the yard to make sure that they were not close to the house.

Still unsettled by the howling, she made her way to her dad's room. She wanted to ask if he heard the howling. As she walked through the darkness of the house, she bumped into a small table in the hallway. She rubbed her knee as her eyes adjusted to the dark. She was almost to her dad's room when she heard a noise. The hair on the back of her neck rose as she listened to the scratching sound. Her breath caught in her throat. There was a scratching noise coming from downstairs. As she continued to listen it seemed to be coming from the front door. Without warning another loud howl echoed through the house. She was paralyzed with fear. Was the wolf at the front door? Was it trying to get in?

She strained to hear if the scratching noise was coming from the front door, but her heart was pounding so loud that it was difficult to hear over the thundering noise in her ears.

Her body grew clammy and her palms sweaty as the scratching continued. She slowly made her way to the stairs. Could she gather the courage to peek outside the small windows that were on the side of the front door?

What if it was a lost dog scared of the howling? Or could it be a kitten missing its mother. She had to know what was scratching on the front door.

As she walked downstairs, a chill ran across her. There was someone on the stairs with her. As the lights came on she screamed, "Dad, you scared me!"

"I am sorry. I heard the howls and then I thought I heard movement in the house."

Lizzy pointed to the front door and said, "Something is scratching at the front door. I thought maybe it was a kitten or puppy trying to get away from the howling."

Her dad stared at the door as he listened for the sounds. Another howl pierced the night. This time it sounded as if the animal was outside the front door. In a shaky voice Lizzy asked, "Is… Is that a wolf?"

Her dad shook his head, "That can't be a wolf. They are not indigent to Louisiana. It could be a coyote, but I don't know if they howl like that."

"Well, Dad, it sure sounds like a wolf howling outside to me."

As they continued downstairs the scratching at the front door intensified. There was almost a panicked sound to the scratching, if that was possible.

Her dad peered out the window by the front door. Not seeing anything he reached for the door. "Um, Dad, I wouldn't do that," Lizzy warned. Unfortunately, it was too late. He had opened the door, and a gust of hot air rushed in from the bayou. The chirp of the crickets filled the night air.

Her dad stepped out onto the porch. They were both surprised to discover nothing there. Looking at Lizzy, he stated, "Maybe whatever was out here heard the doorknob turning and took off."

Stepping out onto the porch with her dad, she looked at the bright moon high in the sky. Wisps of gray clouds drifted over it.

As if sensing their presence the night grew quiet. The crickets ceased their chirping. Even the howling had stopped. Lizzy walked to the edge of the porch where her bedroom was located on the second floor. She stared out into the swamp fearing she would see the glowing red eyes again. All she saw was the outline of the swamp.

As her dad led her back inside, he stated, "Maybe it was just the wind."

"Howling dad?"

Reluctantly, he admitted, "I'm not sure. Let's get back to bed though."

As Lizzy drifted off to sleep, she had disturbing dreams. She dreamed of the wolves howling deep in the swamp. They surrounded the woman from a previous dream and appeared to be bowing in front of her as if waiting for a command from the woman. As if sensing her presence the wolves turned around and stared at her with their glowing red eyes. She took off in a run, praying they didn't catch up with her.

She found herself in the midst of the dark swamp running for her very life. Her feet thud heavily against the soggy ground as the thunderous roar of the glowing red eyed monsters chased after her. She shoved helplessly through the brittle pine trees, leafless branches clawed at her flesh.

As she made her way through the swamps she continued to swat at the limbs reaching out for her, their spindly branches snagging her hair. The howls of the wolves echoed around her.

Her heart pounded furiously in her chest as her lungs grew tight. She feared she would collapse at any minute from sheer exhaustion. An eerie mist swirled around her. They were so close that she could feel their hot breath against her skin.

If they caught her, she was a goner. Frantically, she glanced over her shoulder. She struggled to keep her tired legs moving. She could almost feel them nipping at her heels as she forced herself to run faster. A woman's voice pierced the night, her sinister voice sounded like a thousand snakes hissing in her, "There's no use running."

Her muscles protested, causing her to slow down. A cold breeze swept over her skin as icy fingers gripped her body, yanking her backwards as her bones popped in protest. She tried to scream, but only a soft whimper escaped.

She squirmed, kicked, and fought to break free with every ounce she had inside of her, but it was useless. Her arms and legs moved in slow motion. Her blood grew cold in her veins. The woman from her dreams appeared in front of her. "I told you it was useless. Like I said, you won't escape."

She grinned a grin that sent chills down your spine. Her hollow eyes looked at the creatures, "Finish her off!" she commanded.

The wolf-like men crept out of the trees; their red eyes gleamed hungrily towards her. She screamed as the woman's menacing laugh echoed in the night. Suddenly everything went black.

She woke up disoriented, gasping for air. For a moment, she thought she was still sprawled out on the swamp's damp ground as she waited for the monsters' deathly move.

As her heart raced, she untangled herself from the sheets. Beads of sweat trickled down her skin. She rubbed her tired eyes and blinked a few times, making sure that she was back in her room. She looked around for anything lurking in the shadows. It had only been a dream just like it had been the night before and the night before that. She climbed out of bed; the cold hardwood floor felt good against her bare feet. She peered out the window. The soft pink glow of the sunrise spilled over the tops of the pine trees, gently kissing their tops.

While she dressed, the dream continued to replay in her mind. She wondered if the howls had indeed started back up after she went to bed or if they were just merely part of her dream.

She opened the curtains to her window, allowing the bright yellow sunshine to pour into her room. The sky was a beautiful blue this morning with not a cloud in the sky. As she walked into the kitchen, the remnants of the nightmare left her mind.

After helping her dad clean up the breakfast dishes, she went to rush outside. "Whoa, hold on there young lady. I don't want you going out in the swamp by yourself today. Besides, we have to go into town later on to register you for school and get you some clothes if we need to," her dad said.

Chapter 9

Marie stopped at the steps of the school and looked up at it. She could not wait to graduate. The school was filled with kids who lived to torment others. The only thing most of the girls in her class cared about was which shoes to wear today, and what the latest trend was. You would think they lived in a big city the way they acted.

The familiar smell of old books and disinfectant greeted her as she walked down the hall to her classroom. The hallway was eerily quiet, and her tennis shoes squeaked on the freshly waxed floor. She groaned inwardly when she saw that the door to the classroom was closed. She wondered if someone had intentionally closed the door. There went her chances of slipping into the classroom unnoticed.

As she peered through the small window of the door, she didn't see Mr. Arnold. Perhaps he had stepped out of the classroom for a moment. As soon as she opened the door, Mr. Arnold exclaimed, "Marie Beauchamp, you are late once again."

Marie froze in mid-stride as she felt her classmates' eyes fall on her. Mr. Arnold still faced the whiteboard, but merely instructed her, "Report to the office now. Do not come back without a tardy slip. School has just begun, and you are already starting off with a tardy. Worse, you came in this morning tracking mud through my classroom. If you must play in the swamp, can you please wait until after school?"

As her fellow classmates snickered at the teacher's comment, Marie could feel her cheeks turn red. Some of the flowers she needed only bloomed in the early morning hours, and they needed to be picked at the correct time or they would be useless in her potions. She knew that no one here would understand. She couldn't wait until she graduated and didn't have to worry about Mr. Arnold, or anyone else for that matter.

Once in the office, she signed the ominous tardy book. Her signature had appeared in there multiple times last year. "A tardy slip already this year?"

"Yes, Mrs. Stevens."

"You do know that I am supposed to call your father and let him know you are tardy?"

"Do you have to?"

"Well, since this is your senior year, and school has just begun, why don't I let you go with a warning? But let's not make this a repeat of last year, please."

"Thank you so much. I promise that I will try."

As Marie was leaving, a father and a young girl walked into the office. Something about the girl looked familiar, but Marie couldn't place her face.

Once in the classroom, Marie quickly took her seat and could feel everyone's eyes on her.

"Miss Beauchamp?" Marie could not stop thinking about the young girl she had seen walking into the school office and never heard the teacher ask her the question.

"Um, sorry, sir."

"I'm waiting for you to answer the question."

"Sorry, sir, but I don't know."

The teacher raised his eyebrows, and the whole class watched her in silence. "The question or the answer?"

"The answer, sir." She had no desire to confirm that she had not been paying attention. The last thing she wanted was to be sent to the office twice on the same day.

"Well then, class, can anybody else answer the question?"

As Pamela LaCoste answered the question, Marie found herself once again lost in thought. Could that young girl have been Ms. LeDoux's great niece? As if Marie needed something else to worry with. She has heard the children whispering to each other about the nightmares they have been having.

Marie feared that the Nightmare Witch is up to something, but why has she invaded the children's dreams even more lately?

Chapter 10

The thought of starting a new school this morning had Lizzy feeling nervous. Butterflies fluttered in her stomach. She would be the new student, the outcast.

She wondered how small the school would be since Blackwater Bayou wasn't a big town. Living here was different than the city.

Waving goodbye to her dad in the hall, she stepped into the classroom.

"Class, I would like you to meet Lizzy Bradford."

Lizzy looked at her fellow classmates and had a hard time believing that the whole fifth grade consisted of fourteen students. She had hoped to blend in and not be noticed until she became more familiar with the town and school.

"I would like a volunteer to show our new student around, please."

Several arms went up, but one girl in particular was waving her hand frantically. "All right, Allie, you can show Lizzy around." Looking at Lizzy, the teacher told her, "Lizzy, why don't you take a seat next to Allie."

As Lizzy walked over to the desk, she felt the other students' gaze on her. After class was over Allie told her, "Come on. I will show you where second period is."

While they walked down the hall, Allie asked, "Where did you move from?"

"Kingston, New York."

As they continued to walk down the hallway, other students began to stare at Lizzy. Allie must have noticed her discomfort and explained, "Don't pay them any mind. We don't normally get any new students. You are kind of an enigma here."

"Ugh, I didn't realize how small this school was. I didn't want to stick out here."

Allie gave her a smile, "You are all anyone has talked about since we heard someone had moved into Mrs. LeDoux's house." Leaning in close to Lizzy, she asked, "Is it true that the house is haunted?"

Lizzy looked at Allie, unsure of what she was talking about, "I don't think so. I haven't seen any ghosts there."

"That place looks so spooky. I bet it would be the perfect place to have a Halloween party."

Lizzy groaned when she noticed that Math was her next class. That has always been her worst subject. Where the other class had gone by rather quickly, math dragged on. It seemed like several hours had passed instead of forty-five minutes when the bell rang.

After math class, she had science, and then it was history. After history class Allie pulled Lizzy down the hall, "Come on, lunch is next."

As Lizzy stood in line, she grabbed her lunch tray. When the cafeteria worker placed the meal on her plate, she just looked at the dish. "What is this called again?"

Allie giggled at her expression, "Silly, it is jambalaya."

"Okay, exactly what is this that we are eating?"

"You mean you have never had jambalaya? You have been missing out. It is chicken and sausage mixed in with rice and seasonings. Trust me, it is really good."

When they stepped outside, the sunlight warmed her face. Lizzy loved the fact that skyscrapers didn't block out the sun and that you could breathe in the air without smelling diesel fumes from the buses passing by.

As they walked over to a table, Lizzy noticed the clichés of kids. As she sat her tray down, she felt everyone watching her. Allie plopped down right beside her and started eating. "Well?"

Lizzy picked up a small bite of jambalaya and tentatively tasted it. "It's actually not that bad."

"See, I told you that you would like it," Allie said.

Lizzy had to admit that it was pretty good. It was a lot better than the food they served at her last school.

The rest of the day went by rather fast. When the bell rang, Lizzy grabbed her backpack and rushed outside. Her first day at school had gone fairly well, but she was still ready to return home.

Chapter 11

Looking into the mirror, she noticed a small imperfection. It was a tiny wrinkle, but a wrinkle nonetheless. She needed another young girl. She would need to search through her book of spells. If she could enter their dreams, then surely there must be a way to absorb their youth during that time.

She entered her special room, one which none of her creatures would dare ever enter. This room was that of dark shadows. Its source of light came from the deep blue flames of the hearth. The flames would never be extinguished as long as she lived in this simple shack. They cast flickers of light that danced across the shelves of various size jars and glasses.

Near the hearth stood a pedestal made of bones. It held her most prized possession, a spell book. This spell book was like no others of this world. It was sewn from dried and folded skins. Crude inscriptions were drawn on the cover. The parchment was stained brown and ink the color of dry blood flowed across its lines only from her touch. Scrawled along some of the pages were frightening images of inhuman design; grotesque creatures and twisted scenes of dark rituals.

Her fingers glided over the pages as she slowly looked over the incantations in search of the perfect spell. She smiled as excitement built up inside of her. She ran her finger over the spell once more. "Yes, this may be just what I need."

She looked over her bottles and jars on the shelves. Their labels written in a language only she understood. Each bottle glowed a different color, depending on just what potion or ingredient it contained. Some glowed a brilliant red, some a brilliant blue, others a fiery orange, and some a ghastly green.

She gathered everything that she needed; spider legs, the venom from a snake, lizard tails, warts of a frog and, what... oh no... The spell required the caps of the mushrooms, and, of course, they must be fresh. All that she had were dried mushroom caps. It was hard to obtain fresh caps as they tended to bury themselves when danger was near.

***

While the rest of the sleepy town was waking up, Marie Beauchamp was in the swamps looking for the herbs she needed for her Gris Gris bags. Several more girls at school have complained of a witch coming into their dreams at night, scaring them.

Marie knew it was the Nightmare Witch. She has heard the tales of this evil witch since she was a little girl. The Gris Gris bags she was making would protect her friends from the Nightmare Witch. Her power may be strong, but it wasn't strong enough to penetrate the powers of the Gris Gris bags.

She slowly made her way through the dense undergrowth, searching for the necessary plants. Thanks to her knowledge of the plants that grew here, no petal could escape her sight. What she wanted was an extensive pantry with potions, dried herbs, and other ingredients she would need. For now, she had to make do with gathering what she needed at that time.

Marie looked around and shivered in fear. She had never ventured this deep in the swamp. The life here was all but gone, all that remained was despair.

A noise caught Marie's attention and she hid behind a tree. A beautiful woman was up ahead scrounging for herbs just like her. Marie watched in surprise. Where ever the woman stepped, the ground beneath her feet died. The woman called out, "I know there must be mushroom caps somewhere in the blasted land. Surely not all have died."

Marie placed a hand over her mouth, unable to believe what she was seeing. She has to be looking at The Nightmare Witch. Why did she need mushroom caps? She must be working on a spell, but for what? She had no doubt that it would be used for an evil spell.

Marie watched as the Nightmare Witch broke a twig off of a branch to search through the leaves lying on the ground looking for mushroom caps hiding in the undergrowth.

The woman waved her hand in the air. Suddenly the ground quivered as the roots vibrated, coming alive. They moved through the ground like tentacles. Once her world was revealed, the rumblings ceased and the ground steadied.

After the woman disappeared, Marie walked up to the tree and found where the twig had been removed. Beads of sap oozed from the wound. Marie removed a balm she kept on her, placed her hand on the tree and healed the spot where the twig had been taken. "Hush now it will be all right. She is gone. Can you tell me who she is?"

"I have heard whispers of who she is. She is Chauchemar, the Nightmare Witch. You must go back and stay far away from here. You must run now. Any creature that wanders into her swamp is never seen again. Even the woodland creatures fear coming near this area. Anything living near her dies."

Marie exclaimed, "I know that the Nightmare Witch is up to something. Did you hear anything?"

"She mentioned earlier that she was searching for mushroom caps for her spell. She was mumbling something about needing to reach girls in their dreams."

Marie let out a startled gasp, "That cannot be good. She already torments girls in their dreams. I wonder what else she could be trying."

"She looks as if she has started to age. Her hands looked more gnarled than before."

"I must go back home. These Gris Gris bags will be needed to help stop the Nightmare Witch from any evil plans she may be up to."

The tree warned her, "You must hurry. One of her creatures is fast approaching. It is searching for food and anyone who dares to wander this close to her swamps, dies."

As Marie headed back home, she continued to wonder what the evil witch was up to. Whatever it was, it couldn't be good.

***

As Marie rushed to school, The Nightmare Witch looked through her spell book once more, there had to be a spell that did not call for mushroom caps. Just as she was about to give up, she found the perfect spell. This spell would bring the children to her.

As she read over the list of ingredients, she smiled to herself. *Yes, this one would do just fine.* She needed eye of newt, scales from a snake, fur from a bat, and nail clippings of an alligator.

Chapter 12

It was time to prepare for tonight's ceremony. The Nightmare Witch stepped into the waters of the bayou for her ritual bath. She scrubbed her skin thoroughly with the soap lathered moss until it tingled.

The deep throbbing of the drums began as the sun dropped below the horizon. As she stepped out of the murky water, she donned her white robe and wrapped her long, dark hair in white linen, making sure that her hair stayed hidden beneath the soft fabric.

When she entered the large circle, the drums went silent. The creatures' dark eyes anxiously watched her. The Nain Rouge manning the drums patiently waited for her to acknowledge that she was ready to begin the ceremony.

As her creatures brought the young man to her, she began to chant. Her hands hovered over his body but never touched him. He fell into a trance as she continued to chant the strange, hypnotizing words.

As the transformation took place, his skin melted off and was replaced with fur. Claws sprang from his hands and feet. He screamed out in pain as his bones stretched and his body reshaped.

As the transformation ended, his brothers also took shape and joined him.

Chapter 13

Lizzy woke to the sound of rain hitting the roof. As lightening flashed across her room, she thought she saw a shadow in the corner. Thunder and lightning crackled through the room once more as she turned on her lamp. She groaned when she saw the time. Somehow she had slept through her alarm.

She hated being late for school. She had dreamt of her mother again last night. Whereas her other dreams she could remember more, this time all she recalled was her mom telling her to be careful, that she was in danger.

She woke up crying, and in a cold sweat. She jumped in the shower, hoping to rejuvenate herself. Yet, she still couldn't shake the feeling of dread.

As she rushed around her room getting dressed, a sense of unease washed over her. She swore that someone was watching her. When she looked around, she half expected someone to be in the room with her.

During her classes her mind drifted back to last night's dream. She couldn't shake the feeling that her mom was trying to warn her that something terrible was getting ready to happen, but what?

As she walked into the lunchroom, Megan bumped into her and spilled her milk on Lizzy. Ever since Lizzy started school here, Megan has tortured her in various ways. She acted as if she ruled the school and everyone should kiss the ground she walked on.   Megan was one of those girls who enjoyed causing misery to others.

Lizzy turned red in embarrassment as everyone turned around to look at her. She rushed out of the cafeteria as fast as possible. Tears formed in her eyes as Allie ran to catch up with her.

Allie looked at her as she asked, "Do you think that she meant to spill her drink on me?"

Helping Lizzy clean the spilled milk, Allie replied, "I am positive. Megan can be so mean at times, and she is probably jealous of you. You are the new girl, but everyone seems to like you which just makes her dislike you even more."

As the two friends walked to the bathroom, Lizzy hoped her face wasn't as red as her shirt. She has never been so embarrassed. "But I don't understand. I have always tried to be nice to her."

Stepping into the bathroom, Allie replied, "It doesn't matter. You are a threat to Megan's superiority here. Up until now she has been the only one who lived in a big house. She has been the only one who could talk about all the different places she has seen. Now there is someone else who has done even more than her, and it upsets her."

Looking in the mirror at her shirt Lizzy winced. "Ugh, I am going to smell for the rest of the day." The once vibrant red shirt was darkening from where the milk was quickly drying in the Louisiana heat.

Allie searched through her backpack until she found her gym shirt. "Here, you can wear this for now if you want."

Taking the shirt from her friend, Lizzy removed her shirt and slipped the other over her head. Lizzy was so glad that she and Allie became such good friends. They were very much alike in personality, but that was about it. Where Lizzy had fair skin, Allie had the prettiest caramel colored skin Lizzy has ever seen. Lizzy had plain brown hair and eyes that could never seem to make up their mind as to what color they were. Allie had the prettiest brown eyes, they were such a rich brown they reminded her of chocolate. Where Lizzy's hair was straight as a board, her friend's hair flowed down her back in gorgeous waves.

Now both girls were more tomboy than girlie. They both loved P.E. and any sports outdoors. "Thanks," Lizzie said.

"Don't listen to a word Megan says. She is mean to just about everyone. She even picks on one of the seniors, Marie. She is always calling her a freak."

Lizzy nodded her head, "I have met Marie a few times. She seems nice. I wonder why Megan doesn't like her."

"Megan doesn't like anyone who is different." Looking around the room before talking, Allie added, "Plus there have been whispers that Marie practices witchcraft."

Lizzy laughed at the notion, "That is so silly. Nobody believes in witches."

As the bell rang, Allie pulled Lizzy out of the bathroom. "Come on we need to hurry or we will be late for class." As they rushed to the classroom, Allie confided, "Witchcraft is very much real here in Louisiana. I am surprised you haven't heard the stories about the Nightmare Witch. She was caught stealing children over a hundred years ago. She was hanged for her crimes, but they say she cursed the whole town and if you aren't careful she will come after you in your sleep."

Lizzy swallowed hard as she listened to the story. Should she tell her friend whom she had dreams about a strange woman? Before she could tell her, Mrs. Dawson told the girls to hurry up and get to their seats so class could begin.

Once settled in the classroom Lizzy looked over at her friend once more as she thought about what she had just learned. Allie grinned and waved as the teacher began to talk. Lizzy wondered if what Allie had said was true.

After school Lizzy sat on the bench in front and waited for her dad. The warm air did little to cool her off this hot afternoon. She dropped her backpack to the ground. She was beginning to fear that he forgot about her, when Marie walked over to her. "I heard that Megan has been giving you problems lately," she said.

Lizzy shrugged her shoulders, "I don't know what her problem is, but she said that spilling the milk had been a complete accident."

Marie nodded her head, "I just want you to know that not everyone here is as mean as Megan. If you ever need a friend to talk to you can always come talk to me."

"Thanks."

Marie looked into Lizzy's eyes and said, "No, I am serious. We have a lot in common. I lost my mom a few years back. I know what it feels like."

Lizzy's mom's death had her questioning life and death. Was there a heaven? If so, was her mother there? What about her Great Aunt LeDoux? Were she and her mom together now? Pushing down the sadness she felt over the loss of her mom, she said, "I never even met my mom."

Marie told her, "I was your age when my mom passed away. I still miss her." Changing the subject she added, "I understand you moved into the old LeDoux plantation."

"Supposedly it was owned by a relative of my mothers who left it to me. My dad didn't even know that mom had any family down here."

"I knew your great aunt. Her name was Helen LeDoux. She was a sweet old lady even though most of the people here in town thought she was eccentric. She mentioned other family once, and that was to say that they had moved away, wanting a different life for themselves. She feared that everything she had learned would die with her so she asked if I wanted to learn some of her secrets. She told me in confidence that she believed I had the hands of a healer."

Lizzy looked up at the girl, excited to meet someone who knew the woman who was a part of her family. "I want to hear all about her. My dad never knew about my mother's family. He said that she was always quiet about it."

As her dad pulled up, Marie told her, "One day soon I will tell you more about your Great Aunt Helen. I do believe she would have liked you Lizzy."

***

The bright afternoon sun glared off of the white concrete sidewalk as Marie walked home. She dug in her purse for her sunglasses as she replayed the conversation with Lizzy. There was no doubt that the young girl had the same powers as her Great Aunt. Marie could see it in her eyes and she has a feeling that her powers would soon be revealed to her. She must talk to her before it happened so that Lizzy was not taken by surprise.

As Marie walked down main street, she thought about everything that she had learned from Ms. LeDoux. As the school faded behind her, she passed several of the older houses which comprised the town. She wondered just what went on behind those closed doors. Lizzy was the first girl that she had met who lost her mother early as her. She wanted to take her under her wing, just as Ms. LeDoux had done for her.

As a breeze blew by her, catching dust and fallen leaves on the ground, an uneasy feeling came over her. She scanned the street and her surroundings, looking to see just what it was that unsettled her.

As she continued home, she slowed down. For a second, she could have sworn she heard footsteps behind her. As she neared the edge of the swamps, she stopped. This time she was certain that she heard someone moving in the swamp. They were trying to be quiet, but Marie heard the movement all the same. She peered into the woods, hoping to see something, but all she saw was a rabbit darting out from the underbrush. Shaking her head, she let out a small laugh.

As she neared home, a voice sounded in her mind, "Go inside now." Her breath caught in her throat. She could have sworn she heard Ms. LeDoux call out a warning to her.

Once again the voice sounded in her ears, "Marie, you must hurry. Go now!"

Marie looked around, wondering why she had heard Ms. LeDoux's voice, "Marie, NOW!" There was an urgency in the voice that sent chills up Marie's body.

Footsteps sounded behind Marie, causing her heart to flutter as she let herself into the house. Leaning back against the locked door, she waited to catch her breath and her heart to stop racing.

The apparition of Ms. LeDoux appeared before her. Shocked, she asked, "Ms. LeDoux?"

"Oui, cher. I didn't mean to scare you, but the Nightmare Witch's scouts were following you."

"So I did hear something in the woods."

As Ms. LeDoux's apparition faded, she said, "I am still not strong enough to stay long but be warned that the Nightmare Witch is up to something. I fear that she is after my great niece."

Chapter 14

The night looked breathtaking with the moon's overwhelming presence. It hung so close to the ground that she swore she could reach out and touch it.

As Allison Carter walked along the partially hidden path she sensed someone watching her. She laughed at how silly she was acting. Nothing very exciting happened in this little town. There was no reason to be jumpy. She has walked this way plenty of times at night.

She sped up her walking, anxious to see Jimmy. Her day had been pretty lousy, and a secret rendezvous with him was just what she needed.

Jimmy was the first boy she ever kissed and she couldn't wait to kiss him again. He was the most amazing boy in the whole school. He had a smile to die for and mesmerizing eyes. She has had a crush on him since the fifth grade, but she never worked up the nerve to talk to him. Now, not only had they kissed, but they were dating. They have been secretly meeting late at night down by the bayou for the past month. Her parents refused to allow her to date until she was sixteen, so this was the only way they could see each other. She wished they would bend the rules since her sixteenth birthday was three weeks away, but her mom was adamant she must wait.

When she reached the boat dock, she heard a rustling noise in the woods. Her heart pounded in her chest and she waited. A rush of adrenaline moved through her when she heard another sound, this time closer. "Jimmy is that you?" she called out.

When no one answered, the bedtime stories her Grandmere used to tell came rushing to her memory. Her Grandmere warned all of her grandchildren about the Rougarou that walks the swamps late at night. She always believed the stories were told to keep children safe in bed at night, but as the noise drew closer she worried that they were true.

Suddenly, a cracking sound came from behind her. Now she was freaking herself out. When she turned around, she saw a pair of yellow eyes glowing in the moonlight. A loud crack of a tree limb echoed through the night. Her survival instincts kicked in, and she started running through the woods.

She ran straight into Jimmy, almost knocking him down, "Allison, what's wrong?"

"There is something out there following me." She stuttered without thinking.

"What? Where?" Jimmy turned his head, searching the woods for any movement. "I don't see anything."

"It had yellow eyes that glowed in the moonlight."

Jimmy laughed at her naivety. "That was probably an opossum or armadillo looking for some food." Pulling her to the boat dock he said, "Come on. I've been thinking about you all day."

Just the thought of Jimmy kissing her caused her to forget about the strange yellow eyes.

***

As Allison drifted off to sleep later that night she thought about the way she felt when Jimmy kissed her. Suddenly, a sulfuric odor filled her room. She slowly opened her eyes and looked around. She swallowed back a scream as she noticed an eerie mist crawling up her legs. She watched, frozen in horror as it moved quickly up her body. She tried to shake it vigorously off to no avail. Her pulse pounded deafeningly in her ears as a shiver of fear snaked across her body and cold beads of sweat broke out. She found that her voice could produce no scream as the mist reached eye level. A pair of wicked eyes formed in the mist and stared back at her while the vaporous shape continued to wrap itself around her body in a deathly coil.

Petrified, she found her body no longer obeyed any of her commands. A nightmare of visions and hallucinations gripped her mind as the mist continued to encircle her. As the fog encased her, her skin rapidly wrinkled. An unknown force penetrated her mind.

Time seemed frozen and the torment never ending as the creature engulfed her mind, senses, and finally her entire body. The eyes staring at her seemed to mock her as it released her.

The next morning sunlight rushed through the curtains. She found it difficult to wake up. Her dreams had been filled with terrifying images causing her to wake several times twisting and writhing. Each time she went back to sleep, she waited for the dream to end but instead it continued.

Even now, the images from the dream still lingered. She may be wide-awake but couldn't shake the panicked feeling from her dream.

Try as she may to remember exact details of her nightmare she could not. It was nothing but disjointed images flashing through her mind. The horrific images remained blurred, yet they played continuously in her mind. Taking a deep breath, she was determined not to dwell on the dream. She kicked off the covers and found her pajamas were damp against her skin. Running a hand through her hair, she found it damp too. Covered in a cold sweat, she needed to shower before leaving for school. Groaning, a shower meant she would be late for school. Gathering her clothes she rushed into the bathroom.

When she saw her reflection in the mirror, she thought she was still dreaming. Her heart began to beat wildly in her chest as her mouth went dry. The image looking back at her was that of an old woman, and not her normal vibrant self.

Chapter 15

As soon as Lizzy arrived home, she rushed outside. She has been cooped up all day at school and needed the fresh air. When she lived in the city she never cared if she went outside, but now that they have moved here she couldn't seem to get enough of it. Maybe it was that the air didn't smell like car exhaust fumes and garbage, the air was fresh here. Once she found a spot in the shade, she pulled her homework out. She hadn't been aware of just how much time had passed until the sunlight started to fade as clouds rolled over the sun. Long shadows danced across the area.

As she picked up her homework, a noise in the swamp caught her attention. When she started to walk down the path to see what it was, a gentle breeze fluttered through the trees. The tall ferns that lined the swamp shivered in the wind. The shadows in the swamp grew darker. She heard something rustling in the underbrush up ahead.

She didn't realize that she had wandered this deep into the swamp until she noticed that she could no longer see her house. She considered going back, but the noise caught her attention once more. She slowly turned around in every direction, studying the shadows intently for anyone who may be lurking about. She didn't see anything out of the ordinary, but goosebumps popped up on her arms and legs. A feeling of pure unadulterated terror raced through her body. The feeling came out of nowhere. She felt eyes watching her in the dark.

Once again, there was a noise off to her right. Curiosity won out, and she pushed her fear aside to find out what was up ahead. Suddenly, she stopped as her mouth dropped open in horror. A shocked cry escaped her as she tried to look away from the gruesome image.

In the middle of the path was a hideous pile of fur and blood. Something had torn a deer apart. At first it had been hard to recognize as the image in front of her played more like a kaleidoscope in her mind.

Turning away from the hideous sight, she rushed back home. What kind of animal would tear a whole deer apart? Lizzy rushed off to tell her dad what she has found. He would know what to do. Seeing her Dad working in the yard, she hollered, "Dad…. Dad… You won't believe what I found."

"What? And why are you exploring the swamp alone?"

Kicking an imaginary rock on the ground, she answered, "I'm sorry Dad, but I heard something moving about." Taking a deep breath to help calm her nerves, she told him, "Dad I found a dead deer in the woods. Something had ripped it in half."

Putting his hands on Lizzy's shoulders, his rich, deep baritone voice helped to soothe her jangled nerves. "Honey, I told you that the woods were not only dangerous, but that there is the law of survival out here in the wild."

Nodding her head, she said, "It's just that it is so sad. I thought you said that animals only kill what they can eat.

Whatever did this didn't eat it; it just killed it and left it there."

"That is true most of the time, but perhaps a momma animal killed it for her children and something scared it off."

Lizzy looked up at her dad in amazement. She hadn't thought of that. "Well, we did hear all that howling. Maybe they scared off whatever killed it."

That night as Lizzy lay in bed, she still couldn't get the picture of the poor dead deer out of her mind. Just as she was drifting off to sleep the howls started. Grabbing her blankets she pulled them snugly over her head, hoping she was just dreaming.

Instead of muffling out the noise, the howling became louder. Once again, it sounded as if it was right outside her window. As with the other nights, the howls were angry, deliberate. As Lizzy listened closer to them, she wondered if they did have a more human rather than wolf sound to them. But why would a human go into the woods this late at night just to howl?

Too scared to get out of bed, she squeezed her eyes shut and pulled the blankets tighter around her head. If only she could plug her ears with something so that she couldn't hear the howling. Suddenly her prayers were answered, and the howling stopped. There was nothing but silence.

Breathing a sigh of relief that the frightening noise had stopped, she settled back in bed. Then she heard a noise right outside of her window. Swallowing back her fear, threw her covers to the floor, and jumped out of bed. She peered through her curtains.

The moon was high in the night sky. The backyard shimmered in the silvery moonlight. Pressing her forehead against the windowpane she peered into the yard.

She let out a gasp at the sight of a large creature running towards the swamp. Her mind began to swirl, fatigue and confusion conspiring against any form of reasoning. What she saw didn't make any sense. At first she thought it was a giant wolf, but the creature ran on two legs. It appeared to be all black as it faded into the darkness. Without warning, it turned back and howled into the night air.

Lizzy felt her heart stop for a moment. What she had thought was a man had the face of a wolf. She rubbed her eyes, surely she must be dreaming. This was merely a lucid dream that she would wake up from. Pinching herself hard, she called out, "Ouch."

If she wasn't dreaming then there really was a man who looked like a wolf in the swamp. No, she had to have imagined it. It was just too silly to even consider.

Peering into the darkness once more, she hoped to catch a glimpse of the creature yet again. The darkness of the night had swallowed him up. All she saw was the outline of the swamp. Even the howling had once more stopped.

***

The full moon cast a pale light over the dense foliage as he made his way to his destination. He never noticed as the tree roots reached out and grabbed at him. Even the strong stench of rotting flora that hung heavy in the night air didn't bother him. He walked right past the water moccasins as they bared their sharp fangs. As if in a trance, he walked past the murky water of the bayou until at last he reached his destination.

He stared at the house, waiting to catch a glimpse of its occupants. A sneer formed on his face as he thought about the evil that lurked in the swamps behind this serene home.

Even from here he could hear the loud grunts of the creatures that lived nearby. The low rumblings of thunder announced the arrival of the storm. Dark storm clouds came rushing in and hid the full moon.

When the clouds moved away and revealed the full moon once more, nature called to release him from the confines of his human body. He closed his eyes as he shed his skin and manifested into something nightmares were made of.

As the transformation completed, he let out a long mournful howl. As he called out into the night for his brothers to join him, he caught sight of movement near the house. His amber eyes waited to see if the girl would venture out into the swamp.

Then he heard the beat of the drums signal for the creatures to return home. The timbre of the drums echoed through the night as The Nightmare Witch took her rightful place near the altar.

***

As she raised her arms, the creatures of the night went silent. The swamp and crickets stilled in her presence.

Fireflies hovered about unblinking. The only noise was the beating of the drums.

She surveyed her family in the torchlight. Her Nain Rouge beat on the drums made of dead cat skin. As she entered the circle, her creatures dropped to the ground. Tonight, another man would enter their fold. Her body moved with the beat of the drums. Her feet shuffled, and her arms swung side to side while her head rolled free. The power moved through her as the spirits descended on her.

As the power moved further into her body, her eyes dilated. The Grunch brought her a cage holding the red cardinals. Carefully removing one of the birds, she smoothed its feathers. With one quick slice of the long nail, she opened the bird's chest, and removing its heart. She raised the impotent, warm heart to her lips and swallowed the muscle whole.

She told the young man, "Let's make sure that your fellow Rougarou has another family member to welcome into their fold."

The creatures watched as yet another transformation took place in front of their eyes. Once again, she committed yet another sin against an unsuspecting soul.

***

Those who had no choice but to live here with their families in the small, old shacks that lined the bank knew to turn a deaf ear to the strange rituals being practiced. As hard as they may try, it was impossible to tune out the incessant beating of drums. The pounding rhythm echoed in the darkness of the night. It reached through the thin walls with a simple reminder of just how easily they could be reached, even in the safety of their homes.

The throbbing of the drums called to Maddie; it pulled her from her slumber at this late hour. Throwing the covers over her ears, she tried to go back to sleep. The pounding drums demanded her to obey.

With a soft moan, she slipped out of bed. No longer able to control her movements, she walked out into the night to answer a call that forbid her to ignore. The full moon cast a pale light over the dense foliage. Her unclad feet never felt the briars along the pathway.

The murky scent of the bayou hovered thick in the night air as a sense of foreboding moved in. She tried to alert herself and attempted to shut out the sounds of the pounding drums calling her attention. The drums continued to call her, drawing her deeper into the shadowed swamp. In a trance, she effortlessly walked over the bottomless tombs of quicksand that protected the swamps of The Nightmare Witch.

Her heart beat heavy in her chest. Her mind recoiled in fear as the trees in the swamp seemed to come alive with the sharp claws of their limbs mere inches away from her body. At any moment they could snatch her up and swallow her whole. Instead, she continued on over the brackish waters, moving deeper into the swamp.

On and on she walked until at last she saw a clearing. The flickering light from the torches bathed the area in an eerie reddish glow. Her throat grew dry and her pulse quickened at the sight of the creatures before her.

She tried to stop herself from walking into the circle and instead return home, but her body refused to obey her commands. An icy chill passed over her as the woman in the center smirked at her.

***

When the girl was in The Nightmare Witch's reach, she held out her hand. The deep throbbing of the drums increased in tempo as the girl entered the circle. The Nightmare Witch lifted her arms for silence. On the command, the drums ceased their incessant noise, and the night went quiet. This was a treat The Nightmare Witch had not expected. However, one she would not let go to waste.

She reached out and grabbed the young girl with an unexpected strength. The woman lifted the girl up by the neck and started to breathe in her soul. Right before her eyes, the child aged.

Skin once smooth as a baby's bottom became shriveled and wrinkled like that of a hundred year old woman. As the last of the girl's spirit left her body, she threw the body down. Her group of Rougarou pushed their way to the front of the circle. "Eat my loves. Do not leave behind any evidence."

Chapter 16

Now that she has gathered her ingredients, she added them to her large black iron pot. She stoked the fire before beginning her chant. While the brew simmered, she prepared for tonight. She would soon find out if she could steal a child's soul while they slept.

As she drank the potion, her body transformed into that of a hovering fog, one with glowing amber eyes with barely a slit for pupils. She used her powers to make the fog denser now and spread the mist here and there; she moved towards the small town of Blackwater Bayou.

As the Nightmare Witch neared the small town, she reached out and trailed through the streets with the fog. Soon she could cover almost the entire street. After hovering like this for a while, the fog began to creep forward even more. She observed the houses bordering the marshland. Surely there had to be one which kept a window open. At the third house she found what she was searching for. As she peered inside, she saw a sleeping child of about ten. Her brown curls covered her eyes and spilled over the pillow. She looked so innocent sleeping there. She snuck in through the window and hovered over the child as her human form appeared in the undulating mist. She seized the child, paralyzing her before she could utter a word.

Gripping the child's shoulders, she ordered the child to open her eyes and used the searing stare to penetrate straight into her minds. As she filled the young child's mind with nightmares, she drained every ounce of innocence and goodness this child had in her. Her body went limp; her smooth skin wrinkled like old leather, and a look of pure terror was frozen on her face.

As she left the room, The Nightmare Witch felt her powers grow in intensity. The Nightmare Witch was excited to discover just how well this new spell had worked. If only she had discovered this nearly a century ago.

***

Lisa Guillory called out from the kitchen, "Nancy Renee Guillory, if you do not get up right now, I swear I am going to send your brother in there to wake you up."

Lisa waited another five minutes before looking over at Paul. "Go wake your sister up, please. This is the last time that I will let y'all stay up past nine on a school night."

Paul opened Nancy's door without even knocking and started screaming, "Mom, Mom, something is wrong with Nancy."

Lisa rushed to the bedroom and gasped at the sight of her young daughter. Without thinking, she scooped her up in her arms and ordered Paul, "Go grab my purse and keys. We need to get your sister to the hospital."

As she lifted her off of the bed, Nancy moaned, "Mom, I don't feel so good."

Kissing her daughter's forehead Lisa whispered, "Hush now, we are going to get you to the doctor right away."

Paul held the door open for them and rushed to the car to open the back passenger door also. As Lisa strapped Nancy in, she instructed Paul, "I need you to call your Dad and let him know that we are going to the emergency room."

Lisa drove as fast as she could to the local hospital, but she sneaked glances at Nancy in the rearview mirror. She wasn't sure how she could explain to the emergency room attending that this shell of a body belonged to her precocious ten year old.

Ignoring the ambulance parking only sign, Lisa parked her car in front of the emergency room doors, unbuckled Nancy and rushed inside. "Please I need help. My child is very sick." As Lisa handed Nancy to the young nurse, she observed her daughter in dismay.

The nurse gently placed Nancy on a nearby gurney, "I'm sorry ma'am, but did you say that this is your daughter?"

Holding back a sob, she nodded her head, "When Nancy went to bed last night she did not look like this. She looked like her usual self. She woke up this morning looking like she had aged ninety years."

Without following protocol, the nurse wheeled the gurney into an available exam room, "I'm going to page the doctor right now."

"Dr. Jameson you are needed in the Emergency Room STAT!"

As soon as the doctor entered the room, Lisa barraged him with questions, "What do you think is wrong with her doctor? Will she be okay?"

***

Dr. Jameson examined the girl once more, he found it hard to believe that this child was ten years old; she looked like a miniature hundred year old woman. "I'm sorry, but I don't have any answers for you yet. I won't know anything more until I complete the exam and the lab has the results. I plan on having everything run stat. Please be patient with us."

Dr. Jameson called Nurse Harris over, "Will you show the family to the waiting room while we finish the exam? Also, I need you to draw blood and rush it to the lab. We need the results back ASAP."

As she showed the mother out the door, she replied, "Right away, Doctor."

Dr. Jameson looked at his new patient one more time before beginning his exam. This one might be one for the medical journal. He still found it hard to believe that at one time she looked like an average ten year old girl. While he waited for the lab results, he planned to do some research to see if any similar cases were noted.

Chapter 17

Hailey Anderson stretched in bed and slowly threw the covers off of her. She was anxious to get the day started. It was Saturday and she didn't want to waste a moment of it. She didn't have any homework to do or schedules to keep. She could have as much fun as she wanted.

Late that evening after supper the children were all out playing hide and seek. Hailey was hiding behind a tree and giggled as one of her friends ran right past her.

The children were giggling and laughing when the parents called them back home. Hailey's mom asked, "Do you know where Hailey is?"

Amanda Guillory pointed to the tree where she last saw her friend, "She was hiding behind the tree right over there."

When Hailey's mom couldn't find her anywhere, she panicked. While searching for her frantically, several other parents joined in the search for little Hailey but nowhere could she be found. The mom with tears in her eyes asked, "Where can my little girl be?"

Marie had heard about the missing little girl and feared that the witch in the swamp may be behind this. "I know she is alive somewhere. I can feel her goodness." She tried to summon enough power to find the little girl's exact location. She wished her powers were stronger so that she could find her.

Chapter 18

Sheriff Aaron Benoit should have retired six years ago. If he had, then he would be collecting his pension and fishing. He was past his prime. His bones ached and his stiff joints sounded like firecrackers every time he stepped out of his patrol car.

Yet, he could never find it in himself to quit. Now, as they searched for the missing girl, he regretted his decision. He feared that he would have to tell the parents their child would never return home. The swamp could be cruel, never returning those lost in its depths. There were pools of quicksand that a child could easily fall into, as well as other hidden dangers.

What made it worse was the old wives' tales being told. It wouldn't take long before fear of the unknown gripped this small town.

However, as they searched through swamps he found himself replaying the old wives' tales in his mind. The deeper they moved into the swamps it felt as if the trees seemed to watch you, the wind carried with it a menacing cackle, and the shadows moved with the trees.

With each step he took, his mind traveled to darker places. No matter how many times he told himself that the stories were told to stop children from wandering into the swamp at night, he could not banish the fear growing inside of him.

As the sun transformed into a blurry orange memory in the sky, he saw a strange movement to the left of him. A shapeless shadow that he couldn't quite make out. Could that be the young girl they were searching for?

When he walked near where he saw the movement, he noticed a few stray branches twisting in the wind. Nightfall would soon be here and he was eager to be clear of the swamp before then. They would have to continue the search come morning.

This particular area had a menacing appearance. The ground took on a nightmarish manifestation. The trees were reminiscent of hunchbacked ogres with ugly gnarled arms that twisted through the air and massive roots which snaked underground.

From the shadows stepped a beautiful woman. "Ma'am, you haven't seen a child have you? A little girl went missing."

"There aren't any children here. This place is too dangerous for a child."

From the distance Sheriff Benoit heard the other members of his search party calling and yelled back, "I'm coming. It was a false lead."

"Well, thank you for your time." Reaching into his breast pocket, he removed a business card, "If you see her, please give me a call."

"Oh, but I didn't say that I didn't see her. I said there are no children here. There is only death here."

Suddenly four tree limbs from up above reached out and grabbed him. With the flick of a wrist, the Nightmare Witch ordered the tree to rip Sheriff Benoit's body in half.

The search party broke through the clearing in time to witness the death of Sheriff Benoit. Before the men could react, roots snaked out of the ground. The trees swallowed them whole before even one could utter a scream.

***

Nothing exciting ever happened in Blackwater Bayou and Hailey Anderson's disappearance put the small town into an uproar.

Megan peeked out her bedroom window and watched as the news reporter stood outside Hailey's house, waiting for someone to emerge. Several TV news vans lined the narrow street, all wanting to report the same story.

"This is Miranda Simons reporting live from New Orleans, Louisiana. Shock and outrage have struck this normally peaceful, little town of Blackwater Bayou. A ten year old girl has gone missing. Investigators are remaining tight-lipped regarding her disappearance."

Before Megan could eavesdrop further, her mom called out to her, "Megan you are going to be late for school."

As Megan picked at her breakfast, she asked, "Do you think they will find her?"

Megan's mom wiped the counter, scrubbing harder at a nonexistent spill. "All we can do is pray that they do. I can't believe that something like this could happen here."

As her mom drove her to school, she thought about how much publicity the little snot was getting. She had probably gotten herself lost in the woods. It wasn't fair that she was getting all of this attention. She needed to figure out a way to get some of this media attention focused on her.

Chapter 19

As soon as Lizzy arrived at school Allie came running over to her. "Did you hear about Hailey Anderson?"

Shaking her head, Lizzy replied, "No."

In a whisper, Allie told her, "She didn't come home last night after playing hide and seek with her friends. Her parents went from house to house asking if anyone has seen her."

"Do they think she got lost?"

Allie shrugged her shoulders, "No one knows."

From behind the two girls, Megan yelled out, "Maybe the Nightmare Witch got the little brat." Startled, the two friends turned to look at Megan. Megan continued to tease Allie, "Come on Allie you are always talking about the Nightmare Witch and how she will come after you in your dreams. Now here is your chance to prove to everyone she exists."

Another young girl, Gracie Bertrand, interrupted Megan. Of all of Megan's friends, Gracie was the only one Lizzy liked. Lizzy could not figure out why someone as sweet as Gracie was friends with someone as mean spirited as Megan. Lizzy suspected Megan was friends with Gracie because she was jealous of her. Gracie was not only sweet, but very pretty. She has long, dark hair that she kept pulled into a tight pony tail. But what made Gracie so unique were her eyes. She has the prettiest blue eyes that Lizzy has ever seen. "No, it was the Rougarou that lives in the swamp. My grandmere told us that if we don't stay out of the swamp he will get us."

Megan laughed at her friend, "Gracie, don't start that business about the Rougarou again. I'm telling both you and Allie here that our grandparents made up those tales to scare us. There is no such thing as the Nightmare Witch or the Rougarou. It's just plain stupid."

Gracie looked at Lizzy and said, "I am telling you that there is a Rougarou in the swamp. My grandmere says that he likes to eat little children who venture into the swamp. I bet little Hailey Anderson found a good hiding spot in the swamps only the Rougarou found her instead of her friends."

Megan let out an exasperated sigh, "Honestly, Gracie, I don't even know why I am friends with you. You have such childish thoughts at times. There is no such thing as the Rougarou."

Before anyone could continue on with their stories, the bell rang. As they headed off to class Lizzy kept thinking about what Gracie said. She wanted to find out about this Rougarou. She has never heard that word before.

Catching up to Gracie in the hall, Lizzy asked her, "What is a Rougarou?"

Megan pushed Lizzy, "Beat it new girl. You aren't a part of this group."

Gracie looked at her friend, surprised at how mean she was to the new girl. Stepping away from the group of friends, Gracie pulled Lizzy aside, "The Rougarou is supposed to be part man and part wolf. My grandmere said that it lives deep in the swamps and only hunts at night."

Lizzy considered telling Gracie just what she had seen in her backyard the other night, but Megan came over and pulled Gracie with her. "Come on Gracie. We are going to be late for class." Sneering over at Lizzy, she added, "Besides, you don't want to be friends with the likes of her."

Gracie shook Megan off of her, "What is with you, Megan? I am just trying to talk to her."

Megan gave Gracie an ugly look and said, "Well, if you want to talk to the likes of her you can't be friends with me." Megan stomped off without giving Gracie the chance to say anything.

Gracie looked over at Lizzy and apologized, "I am so sorry. I don't know what has gotten into Megan lately. She has been so mean to you."

Shrugging her shoulders, Lizzie stated, "I don't know, but, for some reason, she doesn't like me."

Allie told Gracie, "You are more than welcome to be our friend. I never could figure out why you were friends with Megan."

Gracie told the two girls, "I always thought Megan was one of the cool girls in school but now I am not so sure. She can be so mean to people at times."

As Megan stomped off, she glared back at the girls. Lizzy wished she could get a taste of her own medicine and thought it be hilarious if her panties fell to the floor.

Suddenly, Megan's panties fell to her ankles. As everyone cracked up laughing, Megan ran as fast as she could to the bathroom. *What the fudge???* Lizzy found it strange that Megan's panties fell to the ground just as she thought the very same thing.

As the girls giggled at Megan's misfortune, the warning bell announced two minutes until class.

At recess, the girls found a semi-private area where they could talk. Lizzy asked Gracie, "Do you hear the howls at night too?"

Gracie nodded her head, "I am telling you that is the Rougarou."

Lizzy asked, "You think so?"

Gracie continued, "My grandmere swears that the Rougarou is a man cursed by a witch."

Allie interrupted, "Do you think the Nightmare Witch is the one who cursed the Rougarou?"

Gracie twirled her hair as she thought about the question, "You know I wonder if she did. It would make sense."

As Gracie and Allie continued to talk, Lizzy contemplated everything she has learned. Could the howls at night be from the Rougarou? Could the Nightmare Witch be the one who controls the Rougarou? What about the missing girl? Did the Nightmare Witch have her? Did she order one of her Rougarou to snatch the little girl away from her parents? What about the dead animal? Did a Rougarou kill the deer?

That night, no matter how hard Lizzy tried she could not fall asleep. She tossed and turned, not once finding a comfortable position.

She kept listening for the howls. Instead of howls though all she heard was the storm that had blown in from the Gulf. The wind was so strong that it rattled the windows of the house. Still, she strained to hear if there were any noises carried by the wind.

Just as she drifted off to sleep, the howling began. She jumped out of bed, rushing to the window. Because of the wind, it was hard to determine where the howling was coming from. Tonight, instead of being in front of her house, it sounded far off.

Peering outside, she looked to see if there was any movement in the yard. Because of the storm, it was difficult to see anything in the dark. The moon was hidden by the storm clouds. The rain came down in sheets. This night was not fit for man or beast yet there was undoubtedly a beast roaming the swamps. Was it the Rougarou looking for another girl to snatch from her bed and bring to the Nightmare Witch?

She cracked open her window. Suddenly, another howl shattered the night. This time the howl appeared to be closer. A cold shiver of fear snaked down her spine at the mere thought of a Rougarou being close to her house. As she strained to hear, she wondered if the howling was still far off in the distance and being carried by the wind.

Another howl interrupted her thoughts. No, the howling was closer now. She had to know for sure if a Rougarou was outside of her house. If not, she would never get back to sleep. Pulling on a pair of jeans and T-shirt she walked quietly downstairs.

As she opened the door a large gust of wind came rushing in, pushing her back into the house. The wind was hot and wet from the rain. The steamy air outside reminded her of a sauna. Without warning another gust of wind came rushing in, pushing her back inside once more. For a moment, she wondered if maybe the wind was warning her to stay inside. Stepping out onto the porch, she waited for her eyes to adjust to the darkness. She walked to the side of the porch that overlooked the swamp. Peering into the darkness, she looked to see if she could make out any shapes near the wood's edge.

The storm clouds have moved, and moonlight gently caressed the land. The wet grass shimmered in the silvery light.

Her gaze moved back and forth along the property. So far, nothing stirred. Even the howling appeared to have stopped. Perhaps it had just been carried by the wind.

Now that her fears have been answered Lizzy headed off to bed once more.

***

From the shadows the Rougarou watched as the young girl moved back inside. The old woman who had lived here before had put a powerful spell on the house, one they could not break past, but soon the little girl became curious as to what was howling. Soon she wouldn't be able to resist coming to them in the dark and when she did, they would be waiting.

Chapter 20

The fire crackled and popped in the pit, now and then sending tiny ember flakes into the sky. Most died low in the air, but some danced in the darkness like radiant star bursts blowing in the wind.

Jessica Trahan stared into the fire, her mind clouded from the alcohol she had consumed. She took another long pull from the wine cooler she had in her hands and set the empty bottle by her feet. She looked over at John and asked, "So why do you want to go out in the swamp tonight?"

"Come on babe. Everyone in town is talking about the Nightmare Witch and how she has come back to life. I found a cool costume online and thought it would be fun to take some pictures of you dressed up as the Nightmare Witch out here in the swamp."

"I still don't understand why we have to come out here to do it. We could have done it closer to town."

"No way babe. What if someone saw us? Besides, there has to be some decrepit looking shacks this deep in the swamp."

After Jessica had the costume on, John pulled her along behind him. The deeper in the swamp they traveled, Jessica noticed how flat the breeze was. The pine branches here were barren of needles. Even the water oak and maple trees that could be found in the swamps have lost their vibrancy. "John, have you noticed that this area of the swamp looks dead?"

"It just looks that way because of it being nighttime. The trees are so thick that the moonlight can't get through."

"I don't know John. I don't even hear any animals." As Jessica looked around, she noticed how the trees took on a sinister appearance. They seemed to be bearing down on them, watching their every move. They blocked the swamp, trying to expel any unwanted guest.

Jessica pulled hard on John's arm, forcing him to stop, "I think we have gone far enough. Let's take the pictures here and go back home."

"No way babe. We haven't found an old cabin yet. You don't believe in the Nightmare Witch do you?"

"I just don't like the looks of this place."

As they trudged through the swamp, Jessica glanced into the trees. Then she heard a rustling in the bushes.

An eerie feeling came over her as she listened to the sounds that radiated through the fog. An occasional fish splashed and a big alligator hissed in the distance.

She swore for a moment that the moss dripping from the cypress trees reached for her.

Her breath caught in her throat. Her eyes darted wildly. "What is that?"

"Relax, babe. It's probably a deer."

She let out a startled laugh when a large deer darted across their path. "See I told you," he said.

She couldn't shake the paranoia that next time it would be something far worse than a deer that crashed through the trees. The deeper they traveled into the swamp, the denser the underbrush became. The menacing trees seemed to warn travelers, "Go back. You aren't welcome here."

The moonlight became caught in the trees' branches. What little bit trickled through did little to illuminate the trail. Up ahead, she noticed a strange glow and asked, "What do you think that is?"

Shrugging his shoulders, John answered, "I'm not sure, but the green light would make a perfect backdrop. This may be better than finding an old cabin."

Jessica was relieved to hear that they might take the pictures and then get the heck out of there. The strange light made the swamp appear even creepier. She has heard the stories told about Rougarou lurking in the shadows of the swamp, and then there were the tales of the Nightmare Witch. She knew better than to believe in any fairy tale creatures, but still she couldn't shake the feeling that she was being watched.

Suddenly a figure stepped free of the woods. The woman wore a black cloak that helped her blend into the night. Even though the woman was beautiful, Jessica sensed that there was something strange about her. "Welcome, we rarely get visitors this deep in the swamp," her voice dripped with honey, but her eyes were as cold as ice.

John looked at the woman suspiciously and explained, "We were just out exploring tonight."

"The swamp is a dangerous place to be. Men have been known to get lost here, and never heard from again."

Unexpectedly, they found themselves surrounded by the grotesque creatures nightmares were made of. Jessica tried to scream, but found herself paralyzed with fear. She knew she should scream, run, do something, but she could not move. When Jessica looked at John, she knew they were doomed. He looked at her with fear in his eyes.

Chapter 21

Erica DiMaggio was still unsure about Megan's plan. "Megan, are you sure about this?"

Megan rolled her eyes and said, "Stop being such a big baby. Nothing is going to happen, I promise." Megan was determined to prove to everyone that Marie was behind the disappearances and that there was no such thing as the Nightmare Witch. "I'm going to prove to y'all that there is no such thing as the Nightmare Witch. Are you sure that you have the camera ready to record?"

"It is, but I still don't know about this. What if the Nightmare Witch is real and she comes after you?"

Sighing, she said, "I swear, Erica, you are such a baby. Nothing is going to happen. Just make sure you don't fall asleep and record me while I am sleeping."

Stifling a yawn, Erica answered, "I'm not going to fall asleep."

"Well then stop yawning. I don't want to mess this up."

The two girls joked around and told ghost stories for another hour before Megan announced, "Okay, I think I can try to go to sleep now. Just remember to record me while I am sleeping." Looking up to the ceiling, she called out, "Oh Nightmare Witch, Nightmare Witch, I dare you to try and visit me in my sleep." After calling out her name, Megan informed Erica, "I wish we could have found a little more information on this witch. We can't even call the old hag properly."

"I still don't like this. I think we are messing with stuff we don't understand. What if she is more than a legend and you make her mad?"

"You really are a doofus."

Covering her yawn, Megan plumped her pillow and turned over on her side. Sleep came quickly to the young girl.

As Erica watched her friend sleep, she had to stifle another yawn. Megan didn't say how long she had to record her sleeping, but she hoped it wouldn't have to be for too long. She was sleepier than she realized.

***

Megan had been asleep for maybe an hour when she felt the sweat crawl down the small of her back. When she opened her eyes, she found her room blanketed in a thick mist. Suddenly a loud noise, reminding her of metal being drug across concrete, echoed in the night. The sound caused her to shiver involuntarily. Her nightclothes were drenched in sweat and clung to her body. Terror washed over her when a breath of warm air skirted across her neck.

Before she could scream she found herself in the math classroom at school. All of the chairs were missing and in the middle of the room was a coffin. As she walked over to the coffin, a maniacal laugh eerily filled the room.

Megan wasn't sure if she wanted to see who was inside of the coffin, but she couldn't resist. As she peeked inside, she had to bite back a scream.   Inside was her dead body, but without a stitch of clothing.

As the nine o'clock bell sounded for class to begin, her classmates quickly filled the room. She stood there frozen in shock as they walked right through her body and stood next to the coffin. They were all pointing and laughing at her in the coffin.

A foul smell filled the room; it reminded her of rancid, swamp water. As the children stood there laughing at her, a woman emerged out of nowhere and hovered over the coffin.

"Megan, you called for me?" The woman's hideous breath assaulted Megan's senses, reminding her of rotten eggs.

Her heart pounded furiously in her chest as the woman floated down to where her body lay in the coffin. She stroked Megan's cheek with a long fingernail. A chuckle emanated from the woman as she moved even closer. She gripped Megan's chin tightly, digging her nails deep into her skin, causing her to gasp out in pain.

Megan thrashed back and forth in the confined area, trying to free herself from the woman's painful grasp.

Erica watched in horror as blood started oozing from claw marks on Megan's face. As Megan's shrill cries filled the room, Erica screamed for Megan's mother, "Mrs. Campbell, come quick. Something is wrong with Megan."

When Debra Campbell walked into the room, she feared that Megan was having a seizure. "What happened? Where is the blood coming from? Did she bite her tongue?"

Stammering, with tears flowing down her face, Erica answered, "We were trying to call the Nightmare Witch. I told Megan this would happen."

Megan's mom looked at the scared young girl, and instructed her, "No, this is some kind of seizure. Call 911, please and tell them to send an ambulance here right away."

After about ten minutes Erica heard the ambulance sirens and opened the front door. "Please you have to hurry."

When the first responders walked into the room, they went into action. "How long has she been seizing?"

The Megan's mother replied, "At least thirteen minutes."

This worried both men; typically a seizure lasted only a few minutes at the longest, rarely this long. "What happened to her face? Did she do this to herself while seizing?"

Erica looked at the grownups and informed them, "The Nightmare Witch did it! She was mad that Megan called her a hag."

Megan's mom ignored the young girl and informed the two men, "She was like that when I walked in. The bleeding and cuts seem to be getting worse though."

Both men had to agree, but neither could explain why the deep scratches now covered the young girl's upper body and arms. The gashes on her face alone would need several stitches. "Ma'am, I need to know if your daughter has a history of cutting herself."

"What? No! No, of course not!"

***

As the paramedic's wheeled the young girl out of the house, the Nightmare Witch watched with glee. As a few mottled, brown age spots appeared on her arm, she realized tonight's attack had drained more of her energy than she expected. No matter, she could easily rectify that.

Chapter 22

The following week, another child's parents were knocking on doors from house to house. "Our little girl, Eva, is missing. She went for a walk and has not returned home. Have you seen her?"

Marie was concerned about another missing child. She took a walk in the woods, hoping to find the missing child. Once again, she summoned her powers, but was unable to locate the missing child.

The deeper Marie proceeded into the swamp, the more she became aware of just how alone she was. She should have at least told someone what her plans were instead of heading out alone.

She shivered as a breeze caressed her skin. Here the swamp was alive with life as animals scurried about. The leaves rustled in the wind as the branches swayed.

The day was vanishing before her very eyes. The sunset swirled up ahead in colors of vibrant oranges, pinks and violets.

A panicked feeling overcame her as she realized nightfall would soon be here. She had left her house unprepared, which was not like her. She knew better than to leave without her backpack full of emergency items. Instead, all she thought about today was finding the missing girls.

She walked for what seemed to be an eternity to find the swamp where she had seen the witch, but nothing there looked familiar. She had a feeling that the witch protected

the area with a spell, hiding its exact location from her. She
was certain that she would feel the child's presence, but she
could not pinpoint her exact location.

Hating to admit defeat Marie headed home. She would
continue her search in the morning, but that time she would
come better prepared.

***

The Nightmare Witch had been so pleased with this child
that she forgot her newfound strength and sucked all the
life out of the child. Not caring about the death of such a
young child, she tossed the body to her Rougarou. "Make
sure that you finish her off. You know what to do."

The Rougarou dragged the body deep into the swamps.
They could not wait to eat their tasty food. It didn't take
long before nothing remained of the young child. This child
had been so small that she did not satisfy their hunger.
"We need more of these children," the leader said.

The other Rougarou agreed, "The flesh is so good. Surely
our Master wouldn't be angry if we brought her another
child so soon."

They hurried off to the tiny town, finding an open window
they snatched the child before she awakened. They rushed
back to their master, dropping the young girl at her feet.
"What have you done? We cannot afford to have another
child disappearing so soon. Now what am I to do?" Their
Master yelled.

After erasing the girl's memory, she ordered her Rougarou,
"Now bring her back and do not attempt this again."

Chapter 23

As Marie walked to school, she suddenly found herself surrounded by angry citizens. One of the women pointed at her angrily, "I know you had something to do with these girls' disappearances."

Megan's mom stepped forward, "What did you do to my baby girl? She told me that it was you she saw in the swamp that night."

"Did Ms. LeDoux teach you her witchcraft? Is that how you are getting to these girls?"

Bobby Picou called out, "She made a pact with the devil himself, I tell you. She is bringing him our children."

Sarah Wiggins exclaimed, "No, she made a pact with the Nightmare Witch. She has come to have her revenge."

As Lizzy's dad drove by, Lizzy called out, "Dad, you have to help Marie."

Ted stepped out of the car and heard the crowd hollering. "She's a witch. We have to stop her."

He stepped into the middle of the crowd, pulled Marie behind his back, and yelled, "Have you stopped to listen to yourselves? You are accusing this child of witchcraft and kidnapping. I have seen her with my daughter, and I can assure you this girl would never harm another child." Looking at Megan's mom, he said, "No matter how cruel another child was to her."

***

Deputy Jim Dawson noticed the crowd gathering and decided he better see what happened. With the recent child abductions, tempers were short. Parents were quick to point the finger at someone else, without sound evidence. And since the Sheriff had disappeared, it was his job to keep everything calm in town.

Stepping into the middle of the growing crowd, Deputy Dawson looked at the citizens and said, "I know that we have children missing, but we cannot start a witch hunt or blaming this young girl of harming these children." Looking over the crowd, he continued, "I assure you that this young woman has no connection to the disappearances." Looking at Marie he explained, "Now, I suggest you get your children to school, or they will be late. You need to leave it to the police to find the children." Glaring out over the crowd, he warned, "And if anything happens to his girl, I will know who to question."

As the crowd dispersed, Marie gave him a shaky smile. "Thank you."

Walking over to her, he said, "If any of these people give you a problem, give me a call." Reaching into the breast pocket of his shirt, he pulled out a business card and handed it to her. "No matter what time it is, you can call me."

Ted Bradford opened the front passenger door to his car and told Marie, "Get in. I will drive you and Lizzy to school."

Chapter 24

Lizzy and Allie talked amongst themselves as they waited for the bus. Gray clouds darkened the sky as a brisk wind blew bits of dust in the air. With the missing children on everyone's mind, parents no longer allowed children to walk to school. This morning her dad had to be at work earlier than normal, so Lizzy had to catch the bus. She promised him she would be extra careful and not talk to any strangers, although Lizzy kept it to herself that she knew who was responsible for the missing children. The only problem was that none of the adults would ever listen to her or Marie. It was up to them to stop the Nightmare Witch.

The gray skies did nothing to help her mood either. As she listened to Allie talk about her suspicions as to what happened to the missing girls, Lizzy contemplated letting her know what was going on but decided now was not the time. Besides, she didn't want to put her new friend's life at risk. There was no telling what the Nightmare Witch had planned or what she would do to those trying to stop her.

On the bus ride to school as Lizzy listened to Allie talk about her night, an overwhelming sense of sadness washed over her. She missed having a mother around. All around school, she heard how other girls' mothers brought them out shopping and did things like teaching them how to sew, cook, or even have a spa day. This was things that Lizzy had never experienced. Her dad tried his best, but there were just some things that he didn't consider important, like teaching her how to sew a Halloween costume, put on makeup, or even paint her nails.

The closest thing they had done to cooking was one Christmas they made a gingerbread house, but it turned out so bad that all they could do was laugh at their creation. She wished the bus would hurry up and get to school so she could stop feeling so sorry for herself.

Allie stopped in mid-sentence, nudging Lizzy, "Why the long face?"

Sighing, she answered, "I am sorry Allie. I was listening to you. It's just that I miss my mom."

Allie hugged her friend, "I am so sorry Lizzy. It must be hard, huh?"

"It is at times. I never even got to know her, and now I am living in a house that belonged to an aunt of hers and I never even knew her."

"I am so sorry, Lizzy. I wish I knew what to say to cheer you up."

Shaking her head, Lizzy said, "No, it is okay. Besides, I have my dad and he is great!"

Allie leaned in, confiding in Lizzy, "At least your dad tries. My dad works all the time. We rarely see him and when he is home he is always either on his phone or the computer. Even my mom works, so I only see her at night."

As the bus rumbled to a stop in front of the school, Lizzy forced a smile on her face. She knew that her mom wouldn't want her sad all the time.

Chapter 25

Marie woke up early, way before daybreak. Before going to sleep, she had packed her a backpack with a blanket, plenty of water, and granola bars. She planned to journey deep into the swamp and not stop until she found what she was looking for.

The moon was still out, glowing bright. It sat low in the sky as it waited for the sun to take its place. A few stars still twinkled up above as a chilly breeze blew across her. She ran her hands up and down her arms to ward off the goose bumps crawling up her skin. It was unusual for a chill to be in the air at this time of the year. Unconsciously, she tightened her ponytail as she walked towards the swamp.

Dead leaves swirled around her feet as she moved deeper into the swamp. The woods on either side of her were dark and eerie in the early morning hours. The stench of rotting leaves filled the air. Silvery moonlight broke through the branches and created skeletal patterns along the ground.

A small trickle of sweat formed along her face despite the earlier chilly breeze. There was an uneasiness in the air that kept her unsettled. A sound from deep in the swamp caused her to jump. It was a screech of sorts, possibly an owl she told herself.

A rustling noise up ahead startled her, similar to a small animal dashing through the brush. She shivered as her mind wandered, contemplating all of the things it could be. Ms. LeDoux had told her stories of creatures rumored to haunt the swamps, things that even she had been afraid of.

Through Ms. LeDoux's teachings she learned that there was such a thing as witches. In other areas of the country she would have been called a Wiccan but here in the swamps she was known as a traiteur, or healer. She also learned from Ms. LeDoux how to cast spells, heal with her hands, the importance of herbs and charms and that where there was good there was also evil.

This area was creepier than she had expected at this hour. Maybe she should have waited until sunrise, but she had hoped to find Hailey and the other missing child.

After a while, she stopped to rest when a feeling came over her. "I know I am getting near. This area feels familiar."

As she continued on, she noticed that there was not a living thing in the area. Even the trees and plants appeared to be dead here. This had to be where the witch had been looking for mushroom caps.

The ground became even more uneven, littered with jutting roots, dead leaves, and twigs. The twigs snapped underneath her feet; the sound reminiscent of brittle bones breaking. This has to be where the Nightmare Witch lived. It was definitely creepy enough.

Despite the rising early morning sun the area remained dark, the sun shaded by drooping branches with an even heavier carpet of decaying leaves. The air was foul with the stench of the dying swamp.

An eerie feeling swept over her. She was being watched. She felt eyes on her from all directions.

As Marie pushed on she was sure that she had found what she was looking for. Up ahead, she saw a village. She knocked on the door, and an elderly woman answered the door. "Please, you must help me, I am looking for two missing children," Marie explained.

Rose pulled her inside, "You must go back. It is not safe for you here. The Nightmare Witch is sure to find you and make you one of hers."

"I am in search of the Nightmare Witch. Am I near her swamp?"

The old woman nodded her head, "It is right behind our village, but you must not go there cher. Evil lives there. It is not safe."

"Two young girls have disappeared from my town. I have a feeling that the witch knows where they are."

Rose looked at her with surprise, "Two? But that is not possible. Only one has been brought to us."

Marie cried out, "You have one of the missing children here with you? Quick, you must show me where she is."

Rose placed a gnarled hand on the girl's shoulder, "She is still resting. Her strength is too weak."

"Please, you must let me help her. I am a traiteur."

"You are a healer? Then yes, you may be able to help her. But first I must warn you that she doesn't look like you remember her."

Rose opened a bedroom door and led Marie inside. Marie shook her head, "No, I am sorry, but you must have misunderstood me. I am looking for a small girl of about ten."

"No, cher, this is the child you seek. You see the Nightmare Witch steals our very beauty and youth from us. That is how she preserves her beauty."

Tears filled Marie's eyes as she replied, "Oh my. I am not sure if I can help her, but I will try."

Marie rubbed her hands together quickly. Once they were nice and warmed, she lovingly embraced the child's head and allowed her strength to be absorbed into the child's body. The child slowly opened her eyes, "What happened? Where am I?"

Marie took the girl's hand in hers and said, "Hailey, I will bring you to your parents as soon as I can, but first do you remember anything about what happened to you?"

Hailey shook her head and replied, "The last thing I remember is playing hide and seek."

Before Marie could ask any more questions, Rose held up a finger up to her face. She opened a trap door hidden under a rug and said, "Hurry, you must hide." Fear showed in the woman's eyes as she continued, "Pure evil is close by. If they find you here they will punish us, and kill you."

Marie dropped down in the small hiding spot as Rose quickly secured the door.

She whispered aloud, "I do not see any of the other witch's evil creatures nearby." Suddenly a noise was heard from the border and appeared to be coming closer and closer.

Rose peeked into the hiding hole, "Oh please, do you have any powers that can protect us from whatever is coming this way?"

"I have only used my powers for healing. I can try to protect the village, but I am not sure if I will be successful."

Marie rubbed her hands together and chanted as she placed her hands on the ground, "Colors it is time to fade and blend into the surroundings. Hide this tiny village from the evil that lurks nearby."

***

The entire village disappeared before the Rougarou broke through the fog. The creatures scratched their heads. "I do not understand. I know that the village we bring the old children to is nearby."

The other Rougarou swatted at the creature, "You fool. We must have gone the wrong way. Look around you, there is no village here."

"I don't understand. I was certain it was here."

Growling, the second Rougarou said, "Come on, we have wasted enough time. There is no one here. The Nain Rouge must have been wrong. Stupid, vile little creatures."

Before heading out, the first Rougarou looked around. The creature was sure that this was where the village had been but where could it have gone?

***

After the danger had passed Marie decided to head back to town. Poor little Hailey was still too weak to walk so Marie was forced to leave her backpack at the village so that she could carry her. "I will be back tomorrow to retrieve it. I must go further into the swamp. I am sure that the Nightmare Witch is planning something. I must find out why she is taking these young girls from our town. I also need to find the other missing girl."

Rose told Marie, "When the witch steals our youth, she always brings the girls here to live. She has informed us in the past it is to show that she has some generosity left in her."

Marie looked at the woman and how much she has aged, "If you don't mind me asking, just how old are you?"

"I will be twenty-nine this year. I was abducted from my bed when I was fourteen. There had been times when I thought of going home, but I fear that my parents would not accept me."

Marie nodded her head, "I pray that Hailey's parents will be so overjoyed with her return that they can overlook her appearance."

The old woman lovingly caressed Hailey's face, "She is so young. I fear that she may be the youngest yet who has been brought to our village. It is so sad that she has been cursed with this body."

"I will look through my spell book tonight and see if there is a way to reverse the spell the Nightmare Witch has put on all of you."

Tears filled Rose's eyes as she replied, "I will keep this to myself. There is no reason to get any of the others hopes up just yet. I fear that what is done cannot be undone. The Nightmare Witch's powers are too strong."

***

Just as Marie had hoped, Hailey's parents were so glad to have their precious daughter back home that they did not care about her appearance. Marie promised, "I will do my best to find a counter spell."

Kissing and hugging their daughter once more, they answered, "We are just so glad to have our Hailey back. We are so grateful for what you have done." Taking Marie's hand in hers Hailey's mother informed her, "If you can reverse the spell that is all the better, but if not at least we have our daughter with us."

It wasn't long before someone frantically knocked on the Andersons' door. A frown formed on Marie's face when she saw that it was Eva Bertrand's parents, "Did you find our daughter as well?" Eva's mother folded her hands as if praying, "Oh please tell me you found Eva as well!"

"She was not in the village where Hailey was at. I will return in the morning and search once more."

Chapter 26

The sounds of crickets and frogs from the swamp echoed in Holly's room. She stared at the ceiling, unable to fall asleep. Beads of sweat formed on her brow from the heat of the muggy night. Suddenly a high pitched howl pierced the night, silencing the other noises of the night. Startled, she bolted upright and gazed toward the window. A low fog obscured the ground outside her window.

Only a sliver of a silvery moon hung in the night sky. There was no light to illuminate the dark swamp. All she saw was rough forms of dark gray and black.

A louder howl broke through the night, even closer this time. Her heart raced as the strange howls bounced off the walls in her room.

A call from a lone whip-poor-will startled her. Her Grandmere always warned that the song of a whip-poor-will meant that death was near. *Death for whom?* She wondered. *Hopefully, not someone close to her.*

As she looked towards the bayou, she swore that she saw a dark shadow move. Rubbing her eyes, she tried to erase the sleep. She has heard the stories about a Rougarou that likes to steal little girls from their homes while they sleep. But that had to be a story parents told their children, right? There was no such thing as a Rougarou, was there? Besides, there are all sorts of animals who wander the swamp at night. It may have even been a deer coming to get a drink of water.

She listened intently for another howl. She heard a bull frog croak and something sloshing through the water, but no more howls. Her heart pounded as she continued to peer into the dark night. She felt a warm breath on her neck and turned around. Nervously, she stepped away from the window. She swore something was watching her.

As a figure emerged from the shadows, she began to tremble.

Holly trembled in fear as the wolf-like creatures surrounded her. Then dream changed and she found herself on the ground outside. Her mind was spinning, filled with disjointed, incomplete images. As her heart beat faster the images whirled and revolved faster and faster.

A noise from deep in the swamps caused her to jump with fear. She had no idea how she ended up out here, but her mind told her that she must go, fast. She began running as fast as she could. One foot in front of the other. Right foot, left foot, she didn't even notice that she had no shoes on her feet. She wanted to get home and away from whatever could be lurking in the woods.

Fear became her motivation. She was not sure what she was running from but something deep inside of her told her she was not safe. Her body moved on its own, choosing which way to go. She prayed that she was going in the right direction.

The hem of her nightgown caught on a piece of underbrush and sent her crashing to the ground. Tears filled her eyes as she looked around.

Without warning, the image of an old lady's face flashed before her eyes. A shiver of fear snaked down her spine as even more frightening images flashed through her mind. If only she could scream out for her mom, but no sound would escape her mouth.

The next morning, Holly found it difficult to wake up. When she went to turn off her alarm clock, she screamed when she saw that the hand reaching out from under the covers was a wrinkled, gnarled hand instead of her normal youthful hand.

Quickly throwing the covers off, and rushing to the bathroom, she looked in the mirror and cried. Now she knew that the rumors were true and that the Nightmare Witch could get to you in your sleep.

***

As the Nightmare Witch has been busy preparing yet another spell, a face formed in the blue flames of the hearth. From transparent lips it spoke, "I have come to warn you. You must take heed as your time is closing in. Ignore my warnings and your life will soon perish!"

"My lord, what are you speaking of? Surely no mortal can stop me. I have outlived even the bravest of witches who have set to destroy me."

The possibility that a mortal could destroy her was impossible. She has destroyed any of those she suspected could destroy her in one swift move, reaching them in their dreams where they least expected it. "Who is it, my lord, so that I can destroy her as she sleeps?"

"You already know of her existence. You must waste no time."

The witch's hands gripped the table as she stared into the flames. Not wanting to play any guessing games as to who this person may be, "Please, Master, give me her name so that I may find her."

Her master did not respond. Instead, he merely sighed. Desperate to know more she pleaded, "Tell me, Master, is there no way of stopping my demise?"

"The future is in a constant state of flux. There is no way to predict what can happen. One different step can make a new path."

"So then I can stop her and change the course."

Without answering the mist dissipated. If the sands of time were closing in on her destruction, her Master would soon collect the remainder of his payment for her powers. Fearing that her unchallenged power may indeed be coming to an end, a moment of clarity came to her. Only one remained in the LeDoux bloodline that could ruin her. Her powers have yet to develop fully. She must destroy her before it is too late.

There were too many years of carefully plotted triumphs to let a mere wisp of a child destroy her.

Chapter 27

Lizzy woke up screaming, thrashing about as the tumultuous nightmare lingered in her mind. Her heart raced as a cold sweat drenched her body. She sat in a state of shock, hyperventilating and desperately trying to forget what she had just experienced. It had seemed so real, the piercing yellow eyes and the vile stench of the creature's breath.

Her neck still hurt from where the creature had bitten her. Her arms stung from where the creature's nails sank deep into her skin. She slowly looked around only to find that her room looked the same as it did when she went to bed.

She told herself once more than it was nothing but a dream, a nightmare actually. If she kept repeating it maybe, just maybe, she would believe that it had been just a dream.

She tried to fall asleep, but every time she closed her eyes, she saw those eyes staring at her in the darkness. Throwing the covers back, she eased out of bed. Marie had given her a Gris Gris bag, but she had forgotten about it until now. She mentioned that it would keep the Nightmare Witch away. Lizzy wasn't certain that it would work, but it couldn't hurt.

She held it tight in her hand as she drifted back to sleep. Although she slept fitfully, the nightmares did not come back.

She wasn't sure how long the alarm had been going off. Her dad knocked on the door and said, "Come on sleepy head, you are going to be late."

"I'm getting up." As Lizzy showered, images of last night's nightmare continued to play in her mind. As she was blow drying her hair, she gasped. Leaning in closer to the mirror, she inspected the bruise on her neck. She turned around and bit back a scream. Long, deep gashes marred the back of her arms, just as in her dream. Her heart was now pounding as she realized that her nightmare had been real. Thoughts rushed through her head. *"Just what happened? How could this be?"*

If she showed anyone they wouldn't believe her, some might even suggest that she did it to herself. She walked into her closet to find something that would cover both her neck and arms.

On the way home from school, she stopped by Marie's house. She hoped that she could help her with the bruises and scratches. All day they had burned, a constant reminder that what had happened last night had been real.

For a moment, she feared telling Marie. However, as soon as Marie saw her, she pulled Lizzy inside. "She came to visit you last night didn't she?"

Relief washed over Lizzy as she asked, "I am not going crazy am I?"

Shaking her head, Marie answered, "No, she is very much real. I believe she is responsible for the missing children."

"Then Allie was right, the witch does visit you in your dreams? She is more than a fairy tale, isn't she?"

"How I wish she were just a fairy tale. I have been combing through the spell books, searching for a way to stop her."

It was then that Marie noticed Lizzy was wearing the Gris Gris bag around her neck. "This didn't work last night?"

"I only thought of it after she attacked me. I held it tight in my hand and slept a little better, but in my mind, I was still waiting for her to come back."

"Hmmm, maybe I need to make it a little more powerful." Walking over to her potions and charms, Marie found a few more items to include in the tiny bag. She placed the bag around Lizzy's neck, and told her, "This should help you better tonight."

"What about the other children in the town? Will the Nightmare Witch come after them?"

"I need to gather more herbs to make extra Gris Gris bags. Don't worry, tonight I will place a circle of salt around each house and say a special spell that should help keep her away for this evening."

Lizzy asked, "Why can't you do that to keep her away for good?"

Shaking her head, Marie answered, "No, there is no guarantee that the salt will adequately protect the house which is why I also say the spell. If it were to rain, the salt would be useless."

"If you want, I can help you gather the plants that you need."

"I have to go deep into the swamps and I cannot promise you that it is safe. It would be better for you to stay here," Marie said.

Lizzy informed her, "No, I want to." Taking in a deep breath, she asked, "Could you teach me some of the spells? I know that I won't be as good as you and that I can't do magic, but I promise to do just as you say."

Marie was taken aback by the request, "If you are sure. I'm just not used to someone wanting to learn what I do. I grew up with children teasing me. Telling me that I was a witch just like your great aunt. It did not bother me; your great aunt was the only mother figure I ever knew."

Lizzy shuffled her feet before confiding to Marie, "I need to tell you something. When I wave my arms, things tend to move. I can also make things come to me. If I concentrate really hard, I can also make things start smoking."

Lizzy couldn't explain the things that have been happening to her. Something inside of her makes them happen. She has no idea how they happen though or even what she was capable of doing.

"I didn't think this would happen just yet. You are still so young. I will have to teach you how to control your powers."

Marie closed the shades in her room before pulling out an old book of spells and various potions to go over with Lizzy. "Your Aunt Helen was a witch, just like you and I are. Most of the people here in town called her a witch doctor. What would upset me is how people would whisper whatever rumors they wished, but even though they wouldn't acknowledge her when they saw her in town; they sought her out for potions or other natural remedies. You name it and she would take care of it. She had a cure for upset stomachs to headaches. She also had a way of knowing things before they happened.”

“But witches aren’t real.”

“Oh, but they are. Each witch has a unique power; some use those powers for good while others use their powers for the devil himself.”

Lizzy asked, “Like the Nightmare Witch?”

Marie nodded her head, “Exactly. You, though, are like your Aunt Helen and have several unique powers. People in this town are highly superstitious and believe that anything dealing with the supernatural is evil.”

Shaking her head, Lizzy stated, “I still don’t understand why the Nightmare Witch wants to hurt me. I’m no threat to her.”

“I have a feeling she wants to kill you before your powers come in.”

Pointing to the book, Marie explained, “This book is called a Grimoire. This particular book belonged to your aunt. I’m not sure what your mother may have done with her book or even her wand for that matter.”

Lizzy shook her head in disbelief, “I know that I have never seen anything like this book before. You honestly think my mother had a wand?”

Nodding her head, “Oh yes, I am sure that she had a wand and a book. Your Aunt Helen used to tell me that your mother had been good at brewing up spells and potions.

Your Aunt Helen was exceptional with growing herbs and such. She made sure that I knew what the name of all the herbs was and their use."

"What about my dad? Should I tell him about any of this?"

Shaking her head, Marie explained, "No, right now I would keep this between you and me."

Marie walked over to her dresser and pulled out two long sticks, and handed one of the sticks to Lizzy, "That was your Aunt Helen's wand." Showing Lizzy the wand in her hand, "And this is the wand she gave me years ago."

Lizzy just looked at both wands and waved hers in the air, "I don't understand how any of this is supposed to work."

"The wand really doesn't have any power in it. The power is inside of you. The wand, however, will help you channel your powers. The crystal on the end enhances your magic." Looking Lizzy in the eye, "Your mother's wand and even her Grimoire have to be somewhere with her belongings, unless your dad found them and threw them out, not knowing what they were."

Lizzy shrugged her shoulders, "I'm not sure. Dad doesn't talk about mom much, but I don't recall him saying anything about finding any strange books."

"It would be nice if we could find your mother's Grimoire. I would love to see what spells she had written in the book."

Lizzy flipped through the Grimoire Marie had laid on her bed, "I still don't understand what a Grimoire is."

"The Grimoire is basically an instruction manual. It tells you how to cast spells, what certain talismans, amulets and charms are for, talks about Divination, and how to summon certain powers. Each witch has her own Grimoire where she can write her spells and it is usually passed down from generation to generation."

As Lizzy flipped through the pages, she asked, "So did my aunt know things before they happened?"

Marie nodded her head, "Yes, and you may also. Your aunt used to say she had "perception"."

"I think I may have that ability. Sometimes I can dream about something the night before it happens. It's not all the time, but just sometimes." Leaning in, Lizzy continued, "And sometimes I swear I can feel what people are feeling."

Marie tapped her fingers along the book as she thought about what Lizzy was telling her, "Hmmm, it sounds like you will have empathic powers."

Lizzy swished her hands and made the pages move in the book, "That is one of my favorite tricks."

Marie concentrated on the hairbrush on the dresser and had it move into her hands, "This is called levitation. It can be extremely fun and very handy." Taking Lizzy's hand in hers, "You will have some very special powers, powers that may not be fully revealed for a few more years."

"I still find it hard to believe that witches really exist."

"Unfortunately, as in life there is good and bad. The Nightmare Witch wants to harm you before your powers come in entirely. She will also try to prevent me from protecting the children of this town.”

“I just don’t understand how she already knows about me.”

“As hard as your mother tried to hide your birth from the witch community, I am sure that the Nightmare Witch could sense your goodness. Your Aunt believed that you would have the ability to manipulate, influence and connect with the energies of this world.”

“More now, than ever before, I wish my mom was here.”

“So do I, honey, or at least your aunt. I can feel the change in the air and know for sure that the Nightmare Witch’s powers are strengthening.”

✳✳✳

In the bathroom Marie filled the bathtub with warm water and recited the spell. She sprinkled different cleansing herbs and flowers in the water plus a few essential oils that should help in healing as well as protection. As Lizzy stepped into the tub, Marie continued to recite her spell.

By the time Lizzy stepped out of the tub the wounds on her neck and arms no longer burned. When she looked at them in the mirror, they were healing. Marie prepared a salve for her to apply on the wounds and explained, “Use this twice a day and in no time they will be gone. You may notice oozing from the scratches on your arms, but that is only the rest of her poison leaving your body.”

✳✳✳

As Lizzy walked home from Marie's, she wondered if these were powers emerging inside of her. She wondered what else she could make herself do. Concentrating hard on her home, she felt herself lift off the ground and then transported through the air. When she opened her eyes, she found herself at the front door of her house.

Excited about this newest power, she spent the rest of the afternoon transporting herself to different areas in the house. As excited as she was about this, she also understood that the only one she could confide in was Marie. She would have to make sure her powers stayed hidden from the other kids at school.

Later that night, as Lizzy prepared for bed, she looked over at the candle on her dresser. Curious if she could light it with her mind, she ordered, "Give me light."

Disappointment filled her when nothing happened. Concentrating harder, she once again ordered, "Give me light."

Still nothing happened.

"Give me light!"

Suddenly the candle had a bright flame burning. But it wasn't just that candle, it was the other smaller candles she had in her room too as well as the lights. Curious to see if there were any other lights on, she left her room. As she walked downstairs, the house was bathed in light. Every candle was burning, and every light was turned on.

Knowing that her dad would want to know what was going on, she had to extinguish the flames and turn off the lights.

Holding her hand over a nearby candle, she concentrated at the candle and thought about blowing out the flame, "Extinguish the flame."

One by one the flames stopped burning, and the lights turned off. As Lizzy walked back upstairs to her room, a feeling of overwhelming sadness overcame her. As she climbed into bed, she wished her mom was here to talk to her. "Mom, I wish you could hear me. There is so much that I want to know. I'm a witch just like you."

As she laid her head on the pillow, she wiped away tears that crept down her face.

Chapter 28

The next morning Marie found Lizzy at her front door waiting for her. "I had a feeling you would be going in search of the Nightmare Witch. I believe I know where she lives. One day I was wandering around the swamps behind my house and accidentally stumbled upon her shack." In a more hushed tone, Lizzy told her, "The swamp there is so scary. It is like someone sucked all the life out of it."

As Marie listened to Lizzy describe the area, she realized that it sounded like the exact location where she had seen the witch. "Are you sure that you want to go? It will be extremely dangerous. My powers may not be strong enough to protect us and your powers have not come in completely yet."

Lizzy looked at her amazed and asked, "You mean I will have powers like my great aunt?"

Marie nodded her head, "I am sure that you will. Your aunt had to train me how to use mine, but you will have natural abilities that I will never have. Ms. LeDoux could see something in me and knew that I had powers buried deep inside and helped me nurture those very talents. However, I will never be as powerful as her or you. I will always have to depend on spells and charms."

As they walked deeper into the swamp, Marie noticed that they had to be getting close. "Her powers are growing. The land here is already dying." Marie looked over at Lizzy with concern in her eyes, "You can turn back if you want, but I must try to determine what it is. I know that she is behind the girls going missing."

Shaking her head, Lizzy replied, "No, I will go with you. Besides, I am the one who has seen her shack. What if she has it hidden by a special spell that only allows me to see where it is?" Looking up at Marie, she added, "We are in this together, and I promise I will not let you down."

The closer they were to the shack the worse the land became. The land here has been transformed into something made of pure evil. Marie warned Lizzy, "Be very careful where you step. There is no telling what hides in this swamp."

Without warning, Lizzy stopped Marie, "Be careful. There is a creature hiding behind the tree over there." Lizzy pointed to a large oak tree that has long since died. "It almost looks like a goblin from one of my fairy tale books."

As the Nain Rouge walked from behind the tree, it warned, "You two should not be here. It is unsafe. If the Nightmare Witch or any of her other creatures find you, they are sure to kill you." The creature looked around before moving closer to the girls, "Not all of us are evil. There are a few of us that were turned into vile creatures by the witch, but our souls were too good to be truly turned by her. We hide here at the edge of her land, warning others to stay away."

Marie leaned down and said, "I believe the Nightmare Witch is responsible for several children going missing in town."

"The witch is up to something terribly evil. Her Rougarou have been prowling more than normal."

Marie nodded her head in agreement, "I must find out what she has planned."

With tears in its eyes, the Nain Rouge told her, "I think that the Rougarou has already killed one of the girls that you are searching for. I believe that she put a spell on one of the girls in your town."

"You are sure of this?"

The little creature nodded its head, "I wish we could stop her, but there are so few of us and we are helpless. The witch is too powerful."

Curious as to what comprised her army Marie asked, "Just what has she turned into her evil army?"

"At one time I was a rabbit. The evil witch used her powers to turn the deer, foxes, and other poor creatures who wander into her swamp. Some of the Nain Rouge were at one time my friends. The entire swamp around her shack has been sacrificed for her greed of power and youth."
Looking around, it added, "The witch has ears everywhere.
You must be on constant guard. The Rougarou were at one time hunters or men who ventured onto her land. They are under her complete control and are truly evil creatures."

Lizzy looked over at Marie and asked, "Just how are we going to save these poor creatures and the men who have been turned by the Nightmare Witch?"

"I don't know, but her powers are stronger than mine. I need to look over my spells and find out the best way to handle this." Marie felt overwhelmed. She wished Ms. LeDoux was here. She would know just what to do. Marie did know that it would not be fair to force these creatures to stay trapped in their evil bodies.

"Follow me and stay close." The Nain Roux told the two young girls, "Humans are not welcome here." Suddenly the roots snaked out of the ground, shadows followed their every move.

Before they knew it, an eerie cackling rose and fell, a shivery sound that seemed to come from everywhere. Marie looked around in hopes of seeing the Nightmare Witch. A shadow swept down on them from up above before vanishing. Marie knew that the Nightmare Witch was close by.

Lizzy pointed in the direction of a large oak tree. The black silhouette of a woman was lurking in the shadows. Her long black cloak swirled around her. The two girls stood frozen in terror. Marie felt the witch's power emanating from her. It seemed to pulsate in the surrounding air. Marie knew now that she had made a ginormous mistake by bringing Lizzy out here with her. She grabbed Lizzy and pulled her behind her. As a sudden jolt of power traveled from Lizzy into Marie she looked at the young girl in astonishment. It would appear that Lizzy's powers were waking up from deep inside of her. However, this was not the time for trial and error. Her powers were still raw and untamed. Too many things could go wrong, and their very lives were hanging in the balance now.

With each step the witch took forward, the girls took one step backward. Lizzy watched in horror as her nightmare came to life. Using her free hand, she held the Gris Gris bag Marie had given her tight, praying that it could offer them some protection. Her body trembled with fear at just the thought of what the witch would do with the girls if caught.

As Lizzy gripped the Gris Gris bag, she felt a sudden rush of energy building up deep inside of her. A warm sensation seemed to be focused in the center of her hand. As if on instinct alone, Lizzy took both hands and gripped the Gris Gris bag and chanted words she has never heard before. Marie turned back to watch Lizzy in awe, surprised that the girl knew this particular spell.

Just one look at Lizzy and she could tell that her powers had come to light. The witch must have sensed a change in the air as well because suddenly, without warning, she charged at the two girls. Marie gripped one of Lizzy's hands and chanted the spell as well.

In the blink of an eye, Marie called out, "Now!"

Both girls held out their hands as a white stream of light flowed from them and hit the Nightmare Witch directly in the center of her chest. With a wave of her arms, Marie cast a vanishing spell around them, hoping that it would hold off the witch as they made a run for the LeDoux plantation. As she pulled Lizzy along faster, she told her, "There is a protection spell on your aunt's property. We should be fine if we can make it there."

Chapter 29

Marie recalled the tales Ms. LeDoux had told her about the Nightmare Witch. For the longest time she had believed that the tale was meant to scare children, but after meeting the village of elderly women she knew better.

If she wanted to put an end to this witch stealing children away in the middle of the night and haunting their dreams, she must hunt her down. If she wanted this spell to work though, she would need Lizzy's help. Although her true powers have begun to surface there were more hiding just under the surface, waiting to present themselves. She hoped that between the two of them, they had enough power to defeat the witch.

Marie perused her spell book looking for just the right spell to capture this woman.

Excited that she found a spell that should work, she rushed over to Lizzy's house. She knocked on the door and only had to wait a minute or so before Lizzy answered. "Can we go up to your room?"

Lizzy nodded her head and the girls quickly went upstairs. After closing her bedroom door, Lizzy asked, "What's wrong?"

"I found a spell that should trap the Nightmare Witch, but I will need your help."

For the next couple of hours the girls constructed voodoo dolls from old twine that Marie had found. These should trap the souls of the creatures, but more importantly, that of the witch.

After the girls were done, they rushed outside. Once they were deep in the swamp, Marie drew a symbol on the floor of the forest. She placed a white sage candle in the center. Once she was ready to begin the ritual, she poured a circle of salt before lighting the candle. She held Lizzy by the hands and instructed her, "Repeat everything that I say, and don't be afraid."

She started her chant that would summon the witch and her creatures to her.

A Nain Rouge was the first to come. Then a Rougarou appeared its face fierce and ready to fight. Soon others followed. Marie began to fear that the witch was too powerful to come, but a screeching chant suddenly pierced the night. The old witch was trying to do a counter-spell, hoping to stop them.

Marie changed the tenor of her voice, picking up the pace as the words tumbled from her mouth. Each of the creatures was captured in the voodoo dolls.

The wind picked up around them. The night was filled with the howling of demons as the storm raged. Then, as quickly as the storm started all went quiet.

The demons were gone, the creatures, and witch were no more. What was once blank faces on the voodoo dolls were now that of those trapped inside. Marie quickly entombed the voodoo dolls in a box made of Alder wood.

As they walked back to Lizzy's house, Marie informed her, "You cannot let anyone know about your powers or what we did tonight. Let the people of this town think that I am the only who believes in witchcraft."

As Lizzy went to the bathroom to wash her hands, Marie hid the box in a secret compartment in the old house. She then cast a spell, hoping to prevent anyone from every freeing the witch and her creatures.